MW01135551

A MATTER OF TIME

an inquiry into Love

BARRY GULLIVER

© 2018 by Barron Gulliver. All rights reserved.

Printed in the United States of America.

With appropriate attribution, any part of this book may be used or reproduced for any non-profit effort to grow LOVE in the world,

All other uses require written permission. Permission is not required in the case of brief quotations embodied in critical articles and reviews.

For information, address:

LILT Publishing LLC
220 South Lakeview Ave.
Sturgis, MI 49091
liltpub3@outlook.com

Notes

A Matter of Time

1

A bright flash at the water's edge caught her eye. A peculiar object, definitely not a stone, lay glistening on the wet sand. Her glossy brown ponytail fell beside a tanned cheek as she bent to snatch the object from the cool morning waves. It fit her palm perfectly. All smooth edges and shine, not as heavy as a stone, or as cold; its uninterrupted silvery surface devoid of nicks and scratches. Flipping her hair back she could see herself in its flawless surface. *It must not have been in the sand very long.*

An ordinary looking girl, average height, ordinary beach clothes, ordinary sunglasses on her head, ordinary flip-flops on her feet, and a friendly, open face. Ordinary, but not so plain as to attract attention. Only an alert sparkle in green flecked hazel eyes hinted at the concealed grit, inquiring intelligence, quick wit and nimble mind within.

The "rock" neither slipped nor clung in her hand as she absently turned it. The edges and corners felt almost familiar. *This is really nice. I wonder what it is.* Scanning up and down the empty beach, she realized; *Someone must have recently lost this. They'll be missing it. I'll have to get it back to them.*

"Hello, Suzanne."

Startled, she spun left, then right, looking up and down the beach and into the wooded dunes. *What was that?* It was like a voice but; except for a flock of standing gulls pointing out the direction of the cool, early morning breeze, the beach was deserted. *It must have been the wind or something.*

It came again, "Thanks for noticing. That's a good sign."

Yes, it *was* a voice; a friendly, intelligent voice. Humor lurked in the corners of it; vaguely reminiscent of her older cousin, Jim, but it was disturbing. *This was weird!* Again, she checked the beach, the lake and the rolling wooded dunes. Still; no one in sight.

In Middle School Suzanne reached two important conclusions: 1) Appearing ordinary shielded her from nasty taunts and unwanted attentions of cruel, jealous, or just plain horny classmates, and 2) The best way to win an argument was to avoid it. But now, she was more willing to stand up for herself.

Frightening the seagulls into flight, she shouted, "For noticing what? Sign of what? Where are you? Who's messing with me?" Dropping the rock into her pocket, pulling her jacket tight around her, she spun on one foot, caught her balance and strode up the beach toward the end of the boardwalk.

The most level-headed and practical person in her family, Suzanne would soon begin her sophomore year at Lakeview Consolidated High School as a below-the-radar honor student.

Striding through the cool sand she wondered, *Why were seagulls frightened by my voice but not the other one? I must be hearing things! I've got to get home.*

Maybe someone is using a focused speaker; kind of a reverse shotgun microphone, to focus the sound on me from the woods. But how could they do that out here? I must be going crazy!

"You aren't crazy, Suzanne. I need to talk to you. It's important."

"Listen, I don't talk to voices. How do you know my name? Show yourself – and don't try anything funny or I'll call 911. How are you doing this?" She began walking faster. "Forget it, I'm out of here. Leave me alone!"

"I was afraid of this. Look, I'm sorry; I've gotten ahead of myself."

"You sure have!"

"I'll start over."

"Oh, Lord help me!"

"The 'object' you picked up is our means of speaking from the future to your mind. The technology is well beyond any science known in your time but it's not advanced enough to allow me to show myself. I can't hurt you; I can only talk to you."

"Yeah, right. Like, I'm on Sci-Fi Candid Camera now, right?" She slowed and smiled triumphantly, scanning up and down the beach. "That's right isn't it?"

"Please, Suzanne. This isn't Candid Camera and it isn't science fiction. Some of your science fiction accurately depicts bits of the future I live in but most of it is just bizarre."

Ponytail flying, Suzanne whirled around again, peering. No one near.

"This is too weird. I'm talking to voices in my head. It's ridiculous. This rock is going back in the lake."

"No! Please don't. Keep the rock. We need to talk. We must have your help to save the universe."

"Oh, for crying out loud, give me a break! Ohh, I get it. Maybe my third-grade teacher was right. I can change the world! So can Sally and Frankie and Jean and Merle and Mark and Sophie and every other kid in the class. Ri-i-ight! So, what's new?"

"It's true," said the kind, but increasingly urgent, voice, "Please listen."

Suzanne slowed, then stopped and took the stone from her pocket. Turning it over in her hand she settled onto a familiar large sun-bleached driftwood log. *I can't believe I'm doing this. Maybe I can write a book;* The Day I Met the Future, *or* The Day the Future Came to Mind, *or maybe,* Living with a Crowd in Your Head. *I'm pathetic.*

"Okay, whoever you are; I have to admit it; I'm curious. I've got a lot of questions, but you go first. I'm listening – for now. But no funny business."

"Thank you. I've come from far in the future; about 400 years from now as you would measure it. There are terrible times back there. Everywhere people have settled after leaving Earth, battles rage. They brought their violent ways with them. Disagreements are settled by force. Everyone is afraid. No one trusts anyone. Weapons grow ever more powerful and will soon destroy the universe itself. In fact, in our time, your beautiful Earth is already pretty much a wasteland. It's a sad time. But it need not be so."

"Suzanne squinted into the increasing glare off the low waves, "Very creative. Go on."

2

"In our time, modifying the past is unthinkable and absolutely forbidden. Any attempt to do so can expect the most cruelly creative punishments. Even the greediest and most power hungry have foresworn even studying it. Yet, a small group of us have mastered time and have discovered how to contact the past and see the future. We think the authorities may have suspicions, but they don't know how it's done or how we have, so far, eluded their notice."

The sun, reliably appearing on the horizon, somehow comforted and emboldened her.

"So, you're criminals. And I should trust you? How do you expect to gain anything by being here? I could have you locked up in a lead box," she said, flipping the rock in her hand.

"We're not doing this for ourselves. We've discovered the force working at the core of human life. You would probably call it love or maybe caring. We recognize how it has been misunderstood, twisted and ignored to result in the awful situation we now face. The destructive habits and cultures spiraling out of control here will never happen if we can, in your time, begin a spiral of increasing quality of Love."

The rising sun was getting warm. She unzipped her jacket and lowered her sunglasses onto her nose. "All you have to do is get everybody to be nice? That's already been tried. It seems to be an awfully tough job. You really think you can do it?"

"We know high quality love is a far more productive and satisfying way for people to live. Earlier in your history, when there were less of you, some of you recognized this and, as you just said, began spreading this knowledge. Progress has been made; unfortunately, the work is continually eroded by pervasive human tendencies to selfishness, to separate everything into either good or bad, and to believe only rewards and punishments change things."

"Sounds like you have your work cut out for you."

"Yes, and we're running out of time. We have to do better. Human life will soon spread into the entire universe and be so scattered it will be all but impossible to eradicate the errors now leading towards our violent destruction. While all people are still on Earth, we have to teach them how to live in productive peace and harmony."

"What a lovely idea. And you're going to do that, how?"

"That's where you come in."

"ME!?" Suzanne leapt off the log, looking all around for someone else.

"We need you to learn what we have learned and teach it to the world. We will help as we are able.

There may be danger, but it is beautiful, and pure, and there is nothing more important you can do with your life."

Hands on hips, addressing all points of the compass to be sure she was heard, she exclaimed, "Whoa down, big fella! Do you have a 'Pause' button? You've got quite a story – for a rock. It sounds like every Miss America's dream – 'I'll Save the Universe!'

"Why me? I'm nobody. And what's this about danger? No, I'm not interested. How about I mail you to the UN? They're much better equipped than I am."

A cool off-shore breeze picked up as the sun warmed the beach and the wooded dunes beyond. Breathing heavily, she shivered, rubbed her arms, re-zipped her jacket and sat back down. "I'm just a kid!"

"Okay, Suzanne, danger first. Even though the seed of Love exists in everyone, there are always some who have not learned to nurture it – it must be cultivated. There are some who know of Love but do not trust it, and then there are those who actively oppose Love, usually for what they mistakenly believe to be their own gain. Some early proponents of Love disappeared mysteriously or met untimely ends. Fortunately, it's the nature of Love that it can use anything that comes its way, so those early advocates are okay, and you'll be okay, too. The messages they planted have only grown stronger. Love is powerful, it will triumph, it's only a matter of time, but time makes a huge difference. Right now, the work is going too slowly."

"So, Love is the big deal? You want me to write a song about it or something? That's been tried, too. Why me?"

"At the moment your Love is at an early stage of development, but it is of good quality, as far as it goes. We see you have the courage, the inquiring mind and the character to quickly adapt to this work. You also have the determination and drive that's needed. You can do it."

"Wow! Flattery will get you everywhere. As if! I'm still not interested. But I would like to know more about this 'Love'. You mean like the Hippies back in the 1960's?"

"Ah, the Hippies. You have to love 'em. They began to get the idea, but it turned into mostly romance and sex. Romance and sex can be wonderful previews but they're only sub-sets of the Love I'm talking about.

"The whole story will take quite a while, but you'll like it."

3

"All right; for starters, tell me more about how this rock works, how it got here, and how much you can see. And tell me about yourself. Do you have a name?"

The sun had cleared the haze and the sand was quickly warming. Her shorts and t-shirt would be enough now, Suzanne thought. Resting the stone beside her on the driftwood and standing, she stretched, smoothly slipped out of her sweatpants and jacket and stuffed them into her ample, daisy-flowered beach bag. Applying sun block she noticed people beginning to venture off the boardwalk onto the beach, strolling on the wave-packed sand at the water's edge.

She stretched again, ran slender fingers across her sun-streaked hair, took her wide-brimmed yellow straw hat from the bag, settled it on her head and sat back down. The sun and murmuring waves were working their magic. Absently nestling the stone back into her palm, she suddenly realized there had been no voice for a while. Relieved, she relaxed. *Maybe I'm okay. Maybe I just imagined it all.*

She jumped as she heard, "I'm right here."

"You startled me! Where did you go? Oh, no! I'm talking to a voice in my head again, like its normal!"

"I didn't mean to surprise you. You couldn't hear me because your mind was occupied with other things. Right now, having the stone in your hand helps focus your mind. Would you like me to answer your questions now?"

"Well, okay, but people are coming onto the beach and I won't be speaking if they come near."

"No problem, you don't need to speak out loud, I can hear you."

"Oh, that's scary. Do you hear everything I think about?"

"No, only the things you say to me, although you sometimes talk to me without knowing you have."

"Will other people hear you talking to me?"

"Oh no, as we talked I tuned myself to you. By the way, we don't see into your time visually, but we can know it in considerable detail. No need to worry about your privacy, Suzanne."

"I think that answered part of your questions about the rock. It got here, and works, by P2C2E. First mentioned in 1990 by Salman Rushdie in *Haroun and the Sea of Stories*," P2C2E means Processes Too Complicated To Explain."

Throwing her arms up, Suzanne laughed out loud, nearly tumbling off the driftwood. "P2C2E, I'm going to remember that."

"I'm sorry I can't do any better, but you should know that this morning we did place the rock in this specific time and place, so you would find it. Except for my physical body, it contains a duplicate of all that is me, plus many resource materials we thought I might find useful."

"Resource materials? Like what?"

"Similar to a library, a very extensive library, and a great deal of information storage capacity."

"Steve Jobs would have loved you."

"I suppose he would have but I'm glad to be with you. You asked my name. In my time it's Hugh but you may give me any name you're comfortable with; I hope to be your companion for a long time."

"Hugh sounds fine to me. Are you a scientist?"

"I'm a researcher, so in your time you would probably call me a scientist, although research in our time is much more broadly based than in yours. We seldom study anything in isolation as you do because we have found everything is so interconnected with everything else. You may have noticed glimmerings of that truth in your studies."

"Now that you mention it, Hugh, I have noticed many things that sort of fit together or affect each other. What do you study? I'd like to know more about Artificial Intelligence and people's brains."

"I study human development. It fascinates me the way humans develop from helpless eating machines into complex bundles of skills, knowledge and personality traits."

"You know, Hugh – yeah, 'Hugh' is good – I think I might get to like you, real or not. What do you look like at home? How old are you?"

"Well, I would probably look strange to you. I'm in the middle of a normal lifespan at home. Space travel, and different gravity, atmosphere and seasons have changed our bodies over the last 400 years, but in every other way we are still the same humans as you. I must admit though, I rather like just being me here, and not simply what I look like or what I was when I was growing up."

"Yeah, that does sound nice," Suzanne said, unconsciously hugging herself and rocking gently.

"I must ask again; Suzanne, will you help us?"

"Look, Hugh, I just can't say right now. It sounds like something ought to be done, but I don't know enough about the danger, or this Love you talk about or what I would do. You're going to have to tell me more."

"Sure. As I said, it'll take a while, but right now it seems we're about to be interrupted."

4

"Is this seat taken?" he said, motioning toward the well-worn length of driftwood beside Suzanne.

He was barefoot, pants legs rolled up and a jacket over his shoulder. An even tan and tousled, sun-bleached hair indicated someone accustomed to being outdoors. *Older than me,* she thought, and said politely but without warmth, "Help yourself."

"I'm ready for a break. I guess I've walked, like, farther than I thought. There aren't a lot of places to, like, rest on this section of beach. I live down by Lakeshore and usually walk south from there rather than up this way. This is a nice spot."

"Yes, it is. It's usually quiet because it's quite a way from the boardwalk. Have you lived near Lakeshore long? I don't remember seeing you around." *Why would anyone even remember a guy like this?*

"I've lived down there seven years. When I started Middle School, my folks moved there. Mom always wanted to live near the lake. I, like, work pretty long hours on a charter fishing boat so I don't get around much, but it helps my college fund. I've got a National Science Foundation scholarship for college next fall, but it doesn't cover everything."

Laying his jacket on the log beside him, he added, "By the way, my name is Darrel, but everyone calls me Dare – even though I'm not, like, very adventurous. Do you live around here?"

"I've always lived near Big Pine Harbor. I can't imagine living away from the lake. Where are you going next fall?"

"UW–Madison. They have a good Genetics program. I like Madison, and Lake Monona is next to the campus, so I can get out on the water once in a while. Will you be going to college? Have you chosen a major?"

Flattered, she replied, "I'm thinking of Artificial Intelligence and Neurology down at Northwestern someday; I like being near a lake, too."

"That's an interesting combination. You know, I noticed from a distance that you've been, like, sitting here quite a while. Working something out?"

"Not particularly, just talking to this rock." She opened her hand, showing it to him and thinking, *I'll bet that sounded brilliant. Oh well, maybe it'll get him out of here.*

Dare laughed. "At least it doesn't talk back!" Then looking closer he said, "That's not like any rock I've ever seen. Can I look at it?"

Thinking, *keep your mouth shut, Hugh,* she handed it to Dare.

"Wow! This is seriously cool. It feels really different. It's definitely not a rock. I wonder if it's, like, glass or some kind of plastic. Where'd you get it?"

"At the edge of the water down there."

"I wonder what it's like inside. Maybe we could crack it open."

Standing abruptly, she extended her hand. "No, I like it the way it is. I've got to go now."

"Oh, well, maybe we'll, like, run into each other again." He dropped the rock into her hand. "Hey, I didn't catch your name."

She turned, jammed the rock into her pocket, said, "Maybe," and stalked up the beach toward the boardwalk.

"That's your name? Maybe?" But she didn't seem to hear him. Puzzling, he turned and walked down the beach, checking the waterline for shiny rocks. *Girls are strange,* he thought.

Walking fast, Suzanne said, "You didn't talk to him, did you, Hugh?"

"Of course not. I could have but you asked me not to. He has an interesting mind, though. Why didn't you want me to talk to him?"

"Because I'm not ready to share you with anyone yet."

"Yet? You mean you will share me with someone sometime? Why don't you want to now?"

"I don't know!" She kicked at a stone in the sand. It was much bigger than she thought. "Oww! Maybe they'd think I'm crazy. Maybe they'd be scared of me; I am a little bit right now. Maybe they'd take you away for scientific study; I'm not ready for that either. I don't know!" she said, kicking up a miniature sandstorm. "Don't talk to me!"

5

"Did you have a nice walk, dear?"

"It was okay, Mom. I walked down past that big driftwood log and then on the way back I sat and watched the lake for a while. It's pretty calm today."

"Were many people out? Did you talk to anyone? Lunch is almost ready."

"A couple guys talked to me."

"That's nice. Were they from around here?"

"No."

"Oh. Do you want milk or juice, dear?"

After lunch, Suzanne helped clean up, then excused herself to take a nap. She couldn't sleep. The morning's events galloped through her mind like horses on the boardwalk carousel. Just as she would focus on one, another would chase it away.

The morning started so peacefully, and then Hugh had to show up. I'm curious about him, but it was so weird. Why didn't I just give Dare the rock and let him deal with it? He was so dense it probably wouldn't bother him. But they picked me. Or had they? Maybe I just happened to be there at the right time. Wrong time? Why didn't I want to share Hugh or tell anyone about him? Oh, I give up. She rolled over, gave a long sigh and let everything go.

6

"Suzanne?"

"What? Oh, it's you, Hugh. I guess I fell asleep." She felt in her pocket for the rock. "I am so confused. I don't know what to do. I wonder if I need to see a shrink. Although you are kind of interesting, even if you should turn out to be a figment of my imagination."

"Sometimes doing nothing is best; just being still, watching and waiting, like when a storm comes over the lake. It soon clears up."

"I suppose. Thanks. I can hardly wait.

"Hey, Hugh, if you change the future, how do you know you'll still exist 400 years from now?"

"Ah, yes, that's exactly why messing with the past is forbidden. As much as I'd like to see the results, what I do here will almost certainly create a future that does not include me or those that helped me get here; lots of things can change in 400 years. Even if I did exist, I wouldn't know anything had changed."

"I'm sorry about that. That must make you sad. You're very brave."

"Thank you, Suzanne, but I have no regrets. I don't feel particularly brave. It's pretty simple. I know I can help create a better future and I can't conceive of doing anything else.

"Will you and the rock disappear from here if the future you came from no longer exists?"

"No, the rock and I are now part of this time."

"Well, welcome to my world."

"Thank you, I'm finding it much more interesting than when I simply observed it. I'm glad to be here."

7

Her sky-blue bedroom door creaked as it opened slightly. "Oh, good, you're awake, dear. I'm going to run errands in town. Is there anything you want, or do you want to come along? I'll be stopping at the library."

"Thanks, Mom. It's a nice day, I think I'll sit out on the deck or walk down the beach this afternoon."

"Enjoy, dear. See you later."

The deck was in full sun under a clear sky dotted with cotton ball clouds. Sheep and lambs the Southwestern Indians called them. Sighing as she settled into a deck chair, Suzanne mused, "Hugh, out by the lake you mentioned something about a force at the center of human life. Is that what you were starting to tell me about?"

"Yes, it's never been a big secret but it's so pervasive that its importance isn't noticed; kind of like air. You often call it caring, or love."

"That's it? That's the big deal? Caring? Love? Everyone knows about that. They teach it in Kindergarten, and Sunday School. Everyone knows nothing happens until someone cares."

"Yes, they do, and that's a good thing, but those words mean different things to different people at different times. Someone might care about or love their home, their new shoes, their pet, a book, their family, their country, the weather; almost anything. Caring and love are generally regarded as optional; a nice thing to do, frosting on a cake. They are way more than that."

"Okay then, what is caring, what is love, really?"

8

"Let's try something, Suzanne. You know more than you think. Get that note pad and pencil from your bag and write down words that define caring. What it takes to care well and make something happen. Use words that describe what caring is, rather than what it isn't."

"Okay, I've got some. How about helping? Compassion? Sometimes it takes courage. You have to notice there is a need. Then, actually do something. Oh, and knowing how to do it well is important; there have been some pretty sad Good Samaritan stories. Oops, almost forgot, you also have to decide when and how to help; sometimes caring means just staying out of the way. Oh, I'm getting into this; there are lots of ways to describe caring."

"Keep going, when you run out, we'll organize them."

A light breeze circled the house, carrying the distant sounds of children's celebrations and the fragrances of the wooded dunes around the house but Suzanne, busy thinking and writing, didn't notice.

"Okay, I've got a pretty good list."

"Let's look at it a different way now. Do you see any similarities, things that can be grouped together? It looks like some are action words. Is it caring well if you don't do anything? Would you say Action is important?"

"Absolutely; nothing happens without action. Lots of my words are action words. Yes, and many of the words are about knowing how to do the helping. So, knowing or Knowledge could be another group! Without Knowledge you can't do things well."

"I think we picked the right person, Suzanne. You're doing great. In what group would you put your words like empathy, generosity and kindness?"

"Well, they aren't exactly Action words, and Knowledge doesn't quite fit either. Maybe feelings? That kind of fits. No, they're more like the spirit of caring. Yes, I think that would be it, Spirit. Some of the other words fit there, too. I'm still missing something, Hugh. There are some 'orphan' words left. I think I need another group. No, don't tell me. Let's see, if I care about someone or some thing, I must have a caring Spirit to start with and I need to actually take Action. But to do something well I need information and skills. If I have the Spirit and the Knowledge I can choose what to do, and then Act. Ohhh, choose! Choosing well, not rushing in and doing the wrong thing. I need to be wise. Like, Wisdom! That's it, Spirit, Knowledge, Wisdom and Action. Let me work on this."

Writing fast, flipping pages back and forth, Suzanne didn't notice the shade creeping across the deck.

"There, that's amazing, each word fits into one of those four groups. What do you think? What now, Hugh?"

"Let's take a look."

Suzanne's Groups

Action is the physical effect we can apply or cause. It is:

appropriate	generous	thorough	helpful
courageous	persistent	fun	patient
celebrating	unselfish	kind	resilient
nurturing	skillful	engaged	timely

Spirit is a frame of mind, motivation, mindset, attitude, state of mind, or state of being. It is:

open minded	compassion	selfless	joy
empathy	courage	patience	cool
confidence	tranquility	humility	kindness
tolerance	resilience	peace	strength
forgiveness	sensitivity	respect	modesty
generosity	nurturing	perseverance	friendly
free of guilt	celebration	willing to learn	
honesty (with self & others)		rejoicing in the truth	
courage	accepting (of self & others)		

Knowledge is all information available to us at the moment. It is:

curiosity	sensitive	listening	alert
concern	experiment	smell	interest
gut feelings	inquiring	aware	taste
reading	seeing	memory	seeking
happiness	anger	anticipation	sadness
fear	pleasure	anxiety	intuition
disappointment			

Wisdom is the analytical and creative powers we bring to a situation. Wisdom:

considers all knowledge		cares	creates
knows itself	understands	analyzes	enjoys
is thorough	seeks truth	decides	is fair
looks ahead	finds the basic objective/purpose		
solves problems	is gut feelings	considers options	
is even-handed	finds root cause/problem/issue		

"I see you've added brief definitions, and some words are in two categories, Suzanne. I like that. Now, if you think of some examples of Caring or Love, would your four groups describe them, or is something else needed? Are those four groups separate things?"

"Right now, I can't think of anything that can't be described by these groups, Hugh. It's interesting; to completely describe it, each example needs something from each of the groups. You know, the four categories are just arbitrary divisions of a single thing. I suppose it could even be divided up differently. It's kind of like what you said about research in your time, everything affects everything else."

"So, everything that happens can be described as Caring, Suzanne? Nothing happens until someone cares? What about Love?"

"Just a minute, I want to get some iced tea. I guess you wouldn't want any. Do you get uncomfortable in there? Hot? Cold?"

"No, the physical sensations part of me is still back home. Sometimes I miss it, but not a lot; it was never very comfortable there."

"Oh. I'll be right back, Hugh."

9

Returning through the screen door, Suzanne exclaimed, "I love iced sun tea! It's so refreshing. Do you make sun tea at home?"

"Not exactly; our climate doesn't favor plant life as you know it. Most of our nourishment is manufactured, but some forms are pleasantly refreshing."

"It's getting shady here. I'm taking my tea down the beach." She dropped the notepad into her bag, picked it up, stepped into her favorite flowered sandals, clopped down the wooden stairs, stepped into the soft sand blown up around them and strolled toward the hard-packed waterline.

"Thinking about my groups again, Hugh, it looks like Caring and Love are just different words for the same thing. Or slight variations of the same thing. I think everything that is done can be described as Caring, or as Love.

"You know, 'everything' is an awfully big word. I think 'everything good' is more like it. I need to think some more about that."

Approaching her favorite driftwood log, she noticed the waves that lightly caressed the beach this morning were now coming on stronger; wearing white caps and scrubbing and rearranging the dishwater-blond sand. Expanding cotton candy clouds scooted northeast toward Michigan.

The sun-warmed top of the log felt good against her bare legs; much better than when damp after a rain shower. She shivered slightly just thinking about it and returned to puzzling about 'everything good.'

"You know, Hugh, I think its true nothing good happens until someone cares, but some things are bad. I don't think bad things like being lazy, or mean, or cheating, or stealing happen because someone cares."

"You may have something there. Are you sure there aren't any similarities, Suzanne?"

"No, of course not. They're opposites. That's obvious. It isn't Caring or Love when someone is lazy or mean or cheats or steals. No way; that's bad stuff!"

"Are being lazy, or mean, or cheating and stealing, types of Action?"

"Big time, but they're bad Action."

"Do they involve decisions?"

"Of course, but they're not good decisions, Hugh."

"Do they involve some form of motivation or attitude?"

"Sure, bad attitudes."

"And do they need knowledge to cheat or steal or kill?"

"Duh! Do birds have wings? You're messing with me, Hugh; of course they do. What are you trying to prove?"

"Have some tea Suzanne. Feel the sun. Take a deep breath and let it out slowly."

"Okay, that feels good."

"Let's revisit your Science class. What is cold?"

"The absence of heat."

"You're good. What is darkness?"

"The absence of light."

"Excellent! "What is bad?"

"The absence of good. What? No! Wait a minute! Wait - a - minute. You tricked me, Hugh."

"Into telling the truth."

"How is that the truth?"

"Think about it, Suzanne."

10

"Hi, Maybe. I hoped you'd, like, be here! Talking to that rock again? Has it talked back yet?" Pleased of his wit, Dare laughed loudly until he noticed Suzanne's lips tightening and eyes narrowing. "Oh. Oh, I'm sorry; I wasn't making fun of you. I enjoyed your little joke this morning and . . . well . . . oh, man, can I start over?"

"It's a free country. And my name's not Maybe", she said towards the lake, thinking, *What an idiot.*

"Don't say a word, Hugh."

"Oh, I won't. This is most interesting."

Dare began again, "I really was hoping you'd be here. You're cute, and I've never met someone who, like, talks to rocks. Sometimes I talk to the lake. Could I call you sometime? What's your number?"

"It's in the phone book"

"Great! Oh, wait, I don't know your name. What's your name?"

"That's in the phone book, too."

"Oh, yeah, ahh, right. Well, I guess I'd better be going. See you later."

"Maybe."

Dare turned and scuffed off down the beach. *I am such a klutz. She is so cool. Ah, man, what am I going to do?*

"Well, that was sick." Suzanne shivered, pulled her jacket from her bag and slipped it on, leaving it unzipped.

"Sick? Are you ill, Suzanne?"

"No, I just mean that was a bad experience. And I put my jacket on because the clouds are cooling it off out here."

"You've used the word 'bad' quite a few times lately. What do you mean by 'bad'?"

"Well, just now was bad because that guy is so dumb. He just walked up and thought I'd be thrilled to see him. He doesn't even know how to talk to someone. Then, he barely paid enough attention to figure out I'm not interested in chatting with him. Wrong time, wrong place, wrong guy. He is such a dweeb. He doesn't know anything. I can't believe him."

"That's interesting. What about earlier, when you talked about bad decisions and having bad attitudes, and taking bad actions?"

What about it?"

"Would you make another list? A list of words that define 'bad'?"

"I'm mad enough I can do it pretty fast. I'll start with 'dumb'."

11

Scribbling furiously, occasionally pausing briefly to think, Suzanne wasn't aware of clouds knitting together behind her and whitecaps charging further ashore. When the first cold raindrop hit her notepad, she noticed.

"Time to go."

Sliding her pencil, pad and empty tea glass into her bag, she began jogging toward home. The hard-packed sand near the water was being attacked by whitecaps so she tried to run in the loose sand farther up. That didn't work so well either. The rain came harder. Her feet were spraying the now damp sand onto her bag and all over her legs and she was tiring. Pulling her jacket above her head and hugging the bag to her chest, she walked as fast as she could.

Grabbing the nozzle of the garden hose kept by the small, covered side porch, she climbed the steps, hung her bag on the doorknob, kicked off her sandals, rinsed and dried her legs and feet, hung her wet jacket on a peg and brushed sand off the beach bag. Entering the kitchen, she heard her mother's car rolling into the garage.

"Hi, Mom, did you get rained on? Would you like help with anything?"

"There wasn't any rain in town but on the way back it rained cats and dogs – there were poodles everywhere." Giggling, she added, "Would you help me with these bags. It looks like you got wet."

"Oh, Mom, that joke's so old. I was down the beach and not paying attention. That rain came up fast."

Carrying the bags into the kitchen, Suzanne absently wondered if Dare had been caught in the rain. It would serve him right.

"I'll be in the living room if you want help with anything else, Mom."

The sofa by the deck window always had good daylight for a book so Suzanne settled in, pulled the pad and pencil from her bag and resumed working on the list.

"You know, Hugh, it's been easier to come up with words for bad stuff. Do you think there are actually more words for bad things than good things? I'm going to see if I can organize this list. It'll be interesting to see how these opposites look. There might be an extra credit paper in this. I might make a breakthrough that will make the world a better place. Oh, you've been telling me that haven't you? Well, thanks."

"Maybe. Go for it."

"Look at that, I can use the same Spirit, Knowledge, Wisdom and Action groupings as I did for love, but the descriptive words are, like, opposite of those I used for caring and love. And there are more of them because there is such a broad range of 'bad'. Being lazy and being cruel are both bad but they're very different, so it doesn't seem right to put both in the same grouping. This is more complicated than I thought."

"Are the words really opposite of the caring/love words, Suzanne? Could it be they only seem 'opposite' like heat and cold seem opposite? Could varying quality levels of love account for the varying degrees of 'bad'?"

"That's a different idea. I'm not sure I understand it. You're saying wise, stupid and ignorant are just different amounts of a good thing? I don't know; I'm going to have to sleep on that."

The door to the garage burst open and the pungent odors of wet warm cars blew through the house. "I'm home, Honey. Hi, Suzanne. That was quite a squall this afternoon, wasn't it? Have you noticed the double rainbow over the lake?"

"I haven't!" Rushing out onto the still dripping deck, Suzanne stopped suddenly, gasped and hugged herself. "Oh, it's just gorgeous, Dad. I think rainbow is my favorite color."

12

Suzanne suddenly sat up in bed. "I think I've got it!" Above her shoulder, fiery morning sunlight on the headboard was framed by the eight-paned window in the opposite wall. "This is big! It's the only explanation. It's so simple, but it's so comprehensive! Occam could sharpen his razor on this."

"Hey, Hugh, check this out as I write it down. I don't want to forget this." Suzanne reached over the side of the bed, pulled the pad and pencil from her ever-present flowered bag, sat back against the powder blue pillows propped on the knotty pine headboard and began.

"Only "good" characteristics exist. "Bad", or "opposite", characteristics are simply deficiencies, or lesser degrees, of the "good". An example from the physical world is heat and cold, which seem very different, but variations are just greater or lesser degrees of heat. Other examples are light and darkness, pressure and vacuum, and wet and dry.

"I got that part from you, Hugh, and here's the really good part.

"Any abundance, or deficiency, of one or more aspects of Love is generally named, and mistakenly regarded as a distinct characteristic, implying it is entirely separate from everything else. Even though different degrees of Love have different names depending on the 'quality' of Love present, all are simply Love's variations.

"Love isn't just something nice we choose to do, it isn't optional. It's impossible to not Love. The only choice we have is to Love poorly, or to Love well.

"Love is all we do! We just do it at different levels of quality.

"Isn't that great? I'm going to list some examples to help me remember."

"Suzanne's Examples.

(---- = any level could be present, "avg." = average.)

NAME	RIGHT SPIRIT	KNOWLEDGE	WISDOM	ACTION
Ignorant	----	low	----	----
Kind	high	avg.	avg.	avg.
Careless	----	avg.	low	high
Stupid	----	----	low	----
Nice	avg.	avg.	avg.	avg.
Lazy	----	----	----	low
Wicked	low	----	----	----
Evil	low	high	high	high
Wise	avg.	high	high	----
Divine	high	high	high	high

"I'm so excited, Hugh! It's a little scary. What do you think?"

"I like the way you've organized it, Suzanne, it's a great way to illustrate something most people kind of know but haven't really dragged into the light so they can see it clearly. Why do you say it's scary?"

"It's scary because it seems so big. It seems really important and not everyone knows it. I wonder if I should know something like this. I'm not sure; it's just kind of a gut feeling."

"You're right to be excited, Suzanne, it's important and special knowledge that not many people have, but that's more a problem for them, than for you. Does it cause you to think differently about anything?"

13

"Suzanne, are you awake?" sang her mother. "Do you want to have breakfast with Dad?"

Smelling coffee and bacon, and knowing they were probably keeping company with eggs and sweet rolls; Suzanne tossed the blankets aside and pulled on sweatpants. "I'll be right there!" A weekday breakfast with Dad was always special. Usually he just grabbed coffee and ran.

"What's the occasion, Dad? Aren't you getting a late start?" He was a slender 5 feet 10 inches of muscle from paddling long distances in his lake kayak. His kayaking amused the sail boaters and especially the power boaters, but he was well known on the lake and they respected his space – and him.

"The school principals' annual state conference is this afternoon, tomorrow and Sunday. Tom's picking me up, so I get to have a leisurely start today. Nobody spoils me like your Mom. She tells me you've been busy writing lately. School work?"

"Just some stuff that came into my head. I'm not sure what to make of it."

"Good idea to write it down. You're smart; when you look back at it you'll make sense of it. If you're starting to worry about the future, don't; you'll be fine."

"That might be some of it. Right now, I really don't know. It's nothing troublesome, just sort of puzzling. What are you going to bring me from your conference? I have to ask, or I wouldn't be your little girl anymore."

"Just the usual, a big hug – and maybe a little something else."

"I usually like the hug best; a yellow bus refrigerator magnet from a school transportation contractor just can't compete with that."

"There's Tom. I'll see you all Sunday evening."

"Bye, Dad. Mom, do you want to split the left-over bacon while we clean up?"

"Okay, thanks for helping, dear. I have a Friends of the Library work session all day, so you'll be on your own for lunch."

"Mmmm, this bacon is great, Mom. I'm going to have a BLT for lunch."

14

"I guess it's you and me today, Hugh. What was it you asked me before breakfast?"

"I was wondering if this morning's discovery causes you to think differently about anything."

"It's so big. I'm still trying to get my head around it. I can't find the edges. Let me think about it while I'm getting dressed. I'll be back in a while."

Quickly showering and brushing her teeth, Suzanne dried her hair and dressed in a violet Northwestern shirt, white shorts and purple Northwestern flip-flops. *School pride day*, she thought as she made her bed, *pride is a funny thing.*

Picking up her beach bag and padding down the stairs, she jumped off the last step, throwing her arms wide, announcing to no one in particular, "Ta-Daa! I'm baaack!"

"What do you do when you're by yourself, Hugh?"

"Sometimes I rummage around in my memories, sorting them and seeing how things might fit together, and sometimes I just sort of . . . be still."

"Me, too, but I also like to read. It should be nice out on the deck."

Wiping dew off the deck chair, glancing up at the now clear sky, and sitting down, Suzanne remembered Hugh's question and began, "Knowing everything is Love does change things. Instead of labeling people and seeing them as entirely different, I need to see them as a variation of me – or me as a variation of them; sort of like we're connected to each other. It sounds complicated when I try to say it, but it feels easy. It feels right."

"Even that guy on the beach? Dare?"

"Dare will take a while. Right now, I think I'll work at moving toward the higher quality end of the scale; try to get better at the things I listed. I suspect it'll feel better there. Probably work better, too. You know what? I'm feeling, like, kind of bigger, but lighter. It feels good, so I guess it isn't breakfast fighting back. I wonder what perfect Love would be like."

"Oh, hi Mom."

"I'm leaving, dear. Be sure you have a good lunch."

"Okay, don't work too hard; you have to let the younger members do something, too. Bye."

"Hugh, you already know about all this stuff I'm discovering, don't you?"

"Yes, but it took me a lot longer to learn it. You're a natural."

"Why don't you just dump it all into my mind? You're kind of connected in there anyway and it would be a lot quicker, and probably more accurate."

"It doesn't work that way, Suzanne. Information isn't useful to you until it connects to what's already in your brain. Just dumping information in would be like someone building a high-rise apartment building by piling a stack of individual rooms on the beach. It couldn't be used because there would be no connections between the rooms or to any outside utilities. And, it would soon collapse because it wouldn't be securely attached to the ground around it."

He continued, "Your brain has many threads that connect to incoming information, Suzanne, to secure it and make it useful. There are many attachment points on every piece of information. If information is dumped in big chunks only a few connection points are accessible, so the information isn't very useful and soon fades.

"Many attachment points also mean different people may understand the same information in different ways. I just love the way people work."

"I think you're having fun, Hugh! Actually, I am too, but all this thinking makes me hungry. It must be time for that BLT."

"BLT?"

"Bacon, lettuce and tomato sandwich on toast, they're delicious."

Returning to the deck with her sandwich, Suzanne looked at the lake. "The weekend boaters are starting to arrive. I like the sailboats best; they can't just ram through to their destination, they have to be alert and agile to make use of whatever breeze comes their way. Besides that, they look so graceful working the wind. Oops, except for the little pink sailboard that just tipped over. Now she's got it up again. That was quick."

"You know, Hugh, I'm thinking quality Love is more than what we do; I think the best quality Love is being Love. Ohhh, the sun feels good."

A roaring, spitting, cigarette boat arced past the sailboats and screamed out of sight, leaving behind a spreading wake and a grateful silence.

In the silence, Suzanne asked, "How did you know my name when I found your rock? Could someone else have found you?"

"I hope you won't be offended. You are one of many we watched grow up, so I knew your name. We selected you and placed my rock just as you glanced that way."

"I didn't see anyone."

"Have you noticed how you hardly feel a light breeze when you walk with it at your back, Suzanne?"

"Yes."

"Well, we moved through time in such a way that the breeze of time didn't touch us. If we didn't do it perfectly you may have noticed a tiny flash of light."

"I did! I thought it was a reflection off your rock! Wow, I saw you!"

"How long will your rock last? You said you hoped to be with me for a long time."

"The rock is indestructible so, in a way, I've been immortalized in this form. Sometime in the future I may even learn how things turn out. That would be strange, I would be the only source of information about a future that didn't happen. Do you think anyone would believe me? Or care?"

"Probably not, and that's too bad; you should get credit for what you do, Hugh."

"Getting credit from others is overrated. The good part is just knowing I've done something of value. Right now, I'm feeling pretty good that we picked you."

"Thank you but I've got a lot to learn. I'm far from perfect."

"Don't worry, Suzanne, you'll never be perfect. You should find comfort in that."

"What? I'll never get it right, and I should find comfort in that?" She chomped a corner off her sandwich, savoring the bacon and mayonnaise.

15

Dark clouds were moving fast from the west and sailboats were tacking back to shore on gusty winds.

"Think about it, Suzanne. Will you ever have only positive, compassionate feelings; be rid of every dark or selfish thought, even fleeting ones? Will you ever know everything there is to know and never make a mistake? Do you think you'll someday be able to do everything it would be good to do?"

"Of course not, nobody could. I'd like to get an 'A' in this someday, but I'd still feel bad for the times I messed up. Where's the comfort, Hugh?"

"Why would you want an 'A'?"

"That would mean I'm helping people and making the world a better place. Kind of like Dad helping people learn stuff."

"And who would give out the grades?"

"You should work for the FBI, Hugh, you ask so many questions. I guess the grader could be almost anyone – in the end I suppose it would be me."

"Could you clarify that for me? If you gave yourself an 'A' for doing a really good job you would feel bad anyway? Why would you still feel bad if you got an 'A'?

"Because there would still be things to learn and do; an 'A' doesn't mean perfect."

"But you just said nobody could learn and do everything. Why would you feel bad for not being able to do something that is impossible?"

"You just don't get it, do you Hugh? I'd feel bad because everything isn't good. Got it? Hey, I can talk to you even with my mouth full!"

"Got it. There is a saying, 'We can see farther than we can reach.' It means we can imagine many opportunities and needs but for one reason or another it's impossible to address them all and we feel frustrated and guilty. Is that what you're talking about with your mouth full, Suzanne?"

"Exactly! Frustrated and guilty."

"Feeling guilty? Guilty of what, Suzanne? Why?"

Leaves and dust suddenly swirled all over the sun-bleached deck. Just as Suzanne jumped up, lightning struck in the nearby woods with a nearly simultaneous thunder clap and rain pounded down. She scrambled into the house, covering her bag and sandwich. Pulling the door closed behind her, she leaned against it, gasping to catch her breath.

"I just don't know, Hugh. I'm so confused. I guess I feel guilty for not doing more; I don't know why, I just do. I don't feel very comforted, I'll tell you that."

16

The old-fashioned chrome alarm clock clanged to life on the other side of the room. Suzanne sat upright, eyes wide, then slumped, *Oh, yeah, it's Sunday.* Fumbling blankets off, she clambered out of bed and staggered over to stop the noise. She had learned an alarm next to her bed was too easily silenced and forgotten, especially after a short night.

Sleep had been elusive. She'd been trying to sort out the events of the last few days. Hugh had been useless; ask him a question and he'd usually respond with a question of his own. It was maddening, and finally so exhausting she had fallen into a troubled sleep filled with dreams of being lost and trying to find her way.

"I heard your alarm, Suzanne," called her mother from downstairs, "Will you have time for breakfast before we go to church?"

"Sure, I'll be down in half an hour." Getting ready didn't take long. For the convenience of tourists and vacationers, the early service was "come as you are."

The drive to church was mostly pleasant back-roads with wildflowers and graceful grasses crowding the asphalt pavement, except where tall trees stood guard, or a tidy cottage faced the road. Suzanne always enjoyed the changes as summer slipped past.

Sunday morning church had always been part of her life. She could hardly imagine a week without it, nor could she remember anything specific from previous services. The predictable routine and familiar hymns were comforting.

The pastor's message was about God's forgiveness of sin and enduring love for everyone, which always seemed strange and a little wishy-washy to Suzanne. Realizing she had routinely dropped the rock into her pocket she thought, "Does that seem strange to you, Hugh? It does to me. And there's that love word again. I don't see how all that fits."

Just then, the organ began the closing hymn. *Amazing Grace* was one of Suzanne's favorites and she was carried away in the flow of the music and the poetry of the words. During fellowship time she visited with members she'd known all her life. It was like a family reunion, full of happy noise; everyone greeting visitors or catching up on the lives of their friends.

17

As they approached the small village of Big Pine Harbor, Suzanne said, "Mom, how about lunch at Golden Sands Café? We're a little ahead of the rush; maybe there'll be a table outside and we can watch the tourists go by."

"Good idea, Suzanne. Sunshine, good food, no cooking, no clean-up, and an entertaining show!"

Suzanne ordered a grilled ham and cheese sandwich, house fries and a very-berry smoothie. Her mother ordered biscuits with sausage gravy and raspberry iced tea. They had settled in to watch the sidewalk traffic when, "Hey, Maybe! We've got to stop meeting like this!"

Suzanne cringed, "Oh, hi Dare. Mom, this is Dare, we've talked on the beach a couple times. Dare, this is my Mom. What are you doing in town? No charters on such a nice day?"

"Nope, the bilge pump broke down yesterday afternoon and we can't get parts until Monday. The pump doesn't run often, but you don't want to go out without it. It's tough to lose a Sunday."

"That's too bad. What brings you up here?"

"I've never been to Big Pine Harbor, so I thought I'd check it out. See if all the people are as nice as you."

Suzanne glanced around, and said, "Most of them are nicer. Here comes our food. Enjoy your visit."

"Oh, uh, yeah, maybe I'll see you around. Pleased to meet you, Mom."

Wandering off, confused, Dare thought, *She is definitely not like other girls. What do I have to do?*

Puzzled, her mother said, "You weren't very nice to him. He seems like a nice boy."

"I was polite, Mom. That's more than he deserves."

"Really? What has he done?"

"Nothing, he's just such a doofus. He thinks he's so clever. He's like a big, slobbery St. Bernard puppy. I can't stand him."

"Well, he seems nice to me. Why did he call you Maybe?"

Suzanne shrugged, "Because he doesn't know my name; I wouldn't give it to him."

"Oh. How's your smoothie? Wow, look at that hat! Can you imagine?"

"Are you envious, Mom?" Their laughter formed a harmonious duet.

Down the block, unnoticed, Dare looked back and frowned.

* * * * *

"That was fun, Mom. It's been a long time since we've done a girls' afternoon out. When does Dad get home?"

"I enjoyed it, too. Dad should be home in time for supper; I should probably get it started. What are you doing the rest of the afternoon?"

"It's really nice today, but the boardwalk and beach are always so crowded on Sundays. Besides, I don't want to change clothes. I think I'll just sit on the deck and watch it all go by."

Suzanne arranged the chair cushions, leaned the colorful beach bag against the chair leg and sat down. "Hugh, I've been thinking about never being able to be perfect. It makes me kind of sad because I try to do things right."

"That's all anyone can do, Suzanne."

"I suppose, but I wonder what someone perfect would be like, Hugh. It would be nice to know someone you were certain would always be thoughtful, kind, truthful and supportive no matter what."

"Would you be comfortable with someone that always told you the perfect truth, the whole truth and nothing but the truth, Suzanne?"

"Oooh, sometimes that would sting, Hugh. But if they were perfect maybe they'd always have my best interests in mind – so I guess I could get through it. Yeah, I'd probably appreciate it most of the time. And then, I suppose someone perfect would never make a bad decision because they'd have infinite knowledge of the past and future, and they'd use that knowledge in a perfectly wise way every time. I could definitely get along with someone like that.

You know, Hugh, the beach and the lake out there look like anthills today; people are scurrying around so frantically. I wonder how many are actually enjoying themselves. Some look as though they're trying to get away from something, or hurrying to finish something, rather than enjoying where they are and what they're doing. I wonder if they even know what they're after." She shook her head, "Whatever they're after it's a beautiful day to chase it."

"You were imagining perfect Love, Suzanne. What would perfect Love do?"

"Why do you ask so many questions? I thought you wanted to teach me."

"Well, I figure if you end up knowing more than before, then I've been teaching. Do you know more than before?"

"Well, yeah, I suppose so, but it seems more like exploring than learning."

"I'm glad to hear that; let's explore then. What would perfect Love do?"

"I've got to look at my lists again. Here they are. Okay, to Love perfectly would require a perfectly right spirit, of course. And it would require perfect wisdom, so every decision would be correct. But it would take infinite knowledge to do that. Then, doing everything those decisions lead to would require infinite ability to accomplish anything, and everything, anywhere or everywhere at the same time. That would be a scary person! It is, for sure, impossible to be perfect. What a relief.

I hear the garage door, Dad must be home." Suzanne reached the screen door in two strides and, laughing, called, "Hi Dad, what did you bring me?"

"A hug of course, and I also brought you this book on teacher techniques. They're useful in more than classrooms. They'll be especially helpful someday when you're raising my grandchildren. Let's eat!"

The fragrant late afternoon faded into soft warm evening, then moonlit darkness glistening on the low waves.

18

"Oh, my God! I mean . . ., I mean . . ., Oh, God! No!"

Heart pounding, eyes wide but seeing nothing, Suzanne sat straight up in bed, oblivious to the rectangles of moonlight on her crazy-quilt bedspread. She heard her mother rush up the stairs and through the door to embrace her.

"What's wrong, Suzanne? What's wrong? It'll be all right. I'm here, you're okay."

"Oh, Mom," she gasped, clinging to her mother, "I know who God is! God is Love; I'm not supposed to know God's name – am I? What will happen to me?"

"Of course, God is love, dear. You must have had a bad dream. Lay back down; I'll stay right here until you go back to sleep."

Fully awake and beginning to breathe normally, she realized her mother didn't understand; it would be too complicated to explain now. Suzanne kissed her cheek saying, "Thanks, Mom, I'm okay now. Thanks for coming up," and snuggled back under the covers.

When her mother was gone, and the house was quiet, Suzanne whispered "Hugh, are you awake?"

"Always."

"It came to me while I was sleeping. God is Love! Perfect Love is God! Mom doesn't realize what that means. I wonder who else knows. I'm scared, . . . and awed, . . . and I don't know what else. I know many religions prohibit speaking the name of God, much less, knowing who God is. But I know. Its mind-bending and scary at the same time."

"You seem to be onto something, Suzanne. Talk it out. What does it mean? What doesn't your Mom realize?"

"Mom doesn't realize everything Love really is, much less what perfect Love is. Perfect, infinite Love can do everything, everywhere all at the same time – at church we call that 'omnipotence'. Perfect Love knows everything about the past, present and future – that's called 'omniscience'. All-wise and infinitely caring are also how God is described. God is a perfect, infinite version of everything in my lists. God is not a distant puppet-master we have to fear, bribe and flatter. God isn't even a person that's in one place at a time. God's everywhere; we swim in a sea of Love, a sea of God; God who wants only the best for us. Omigosh, this is huge! It just keeps growing. If knowing this means it's time for me to die, it's worth it, I'm ready to go. It's beautiful! I feel as though I could fly.

"But I'm sad for Mom, Hugh. She knows the words, but she doesn't realize everything they mean. It really hurts. Maybe, with time, I can explain."

Unnoticed, the moonlight had traveled down the side of the bedspread, across the nut-brown floor boards, out the window, across the deck and headed for the shore. The eastern horizon was becoming visible above the lake.

"Suzanne, why would a religion declare the name of God should not be spoken?

"I don't know. It seems like it's just a rule. One reason could be that God is infinite, so any name would limit our understanding."

"You know, Suzanne, some religions say God has many names."

"That's ironic. It could be for the same reason though. God is so big an infinite number of names are needed. Oh-h, my Love lists are like that, aren't they; they only scratch the surface!

"I'm exhausted. Thanks, Hugh. I'll write this stuff down in the morning."

Golden dawn crept into the room unseen as Suzanne melted into a deep, dreamless sleep.

19

Children's laughter, carried from the beach on a light breeze, woke Suzanne. No sunlight shone on the walls or floor, revealing she had slept through the entire morning. Pulling on pink shorts, matching t-shirt and flip flops, she flapped down stairs and found her mother in the sunny kitchen, making lunch for herself.

"Good morning, Mom. Or is it afternoon? I guess I really slept well after you came up. I'm sorry I woke you. Thanks, though."

"I'm glad you were able to rest well. You haven't had a night like that since you were four. You were so upset; it must have been an awful nightmare. Do you remember it?" Over her shoulder toward Suzanne she said, "Would you like breakfast, or lunch?"

"Thanks, I'll make my own." Suzanne said, scooping granola into a bowl and topping it with fresh, fat, blueberries and an overflowing spoonful of yogurt. Sitting down with her bowl and a glass of orange juice, Suzanne took a bite, chewed the crunchy mixture, and hedged, "It's hard to explain. I dreamed I was exploring some stuff and was afraid I was in big trouble for finding it. I was really scared, but I'm not anymore."

"You've been spending a lot of time with your notebooks. Maybe some exercise would help. You go ahead, I'll take care of the dishes, then I'm going to start that Janet Evanovich book I brought home Saturday."

"Good idea, Mom. I think I'll take Dad's kayak out after I write awhile."

As early afternoon shadows eased across the deck, Suzanne recorded her thoughts from the night before, checking with Hugh for accuracy, then said, "Thanks for being there last night, Hugh. It was helpful. My mind is still racing with everything it means. You know, that perfect, infinite Love is God. It's kind of like when we studied physiology in biology class; afterwards it was so different when I saw a person walking or running. I was aware of lungs functioning, heart beating, blood flowing, muscles contracting, nerves signaling and on and on."

Glancing at the softly shifting water, Suzanne expelled a long, slow sigh. "Nothing has changed but everything is different." Standing with a new boldness she exclaimed, "I feel like Christopher Columbus sighting land; it was there all the time, but when he saw it, I think he began to realize how much there was to explore. I'll work on some of the questions later; right now, I'm going kayaking."

Suzanne pulled the bright yellow two-seat lake kayak and a paddle from beneath the deck and dragged them to the water. Severe storms could create four and five-foot waves that destroyed docks, so there were none except at protected harbors. Picking up the double ended paddle she slid the kayak bow-first into the water then, straddling the stern, waded out and dropped into the rear seat. Two strong strokes and she was gliding into a blue infinity of clear sky and calm lake sharing an azure palette that concealed the eastern horizon.

When shoreline cottages became doll houses she turned parallel to the shore and her strokes slowed. Light swells gently rocked the kayak, maybe remnants of a distant freighter's wake, maybe children of the breeze. Small sounds tiptoed out from shore as the sun warmed her tanned face, bare legs and arms. Resting the paddle in front of her, she relaxed, closed her eyes, said, "Solitude without isolation, mm-m-m," and became the sounds and waves and sun.

She didn't know how long she'd been floating but became aware the beach was quiet, the swell felt longer, and she felt cooler. Reluctantly opening her eyes, she realized the sun was completely obscured by thick, high cirrus clouds. In the distance a deep-water fishing boat was outlined against the, now-gray, sky. She watched for a moment then picked up her paddle and turned toward shore. The shore wasn't there! She turned completely around; every direction presented only a gray horizon, and the long, low swell that had lulled her. *Which way was home?*

Planning only a brief paddle in the neighborhood, she had not brought the compass and GPS her father always stowed. Dad would be upset about that. She was seriously lost. *Had she drifted? How far? Which way should she go?*

20

"Hugh, I'm lost, I don't know what to do. Have you got a GPS in there?"

"Sorry, Suzanne, we didn't think to include one because I'm not really equipped for travelling around. If you've got a problem, Love it to death. You're better than you know. If this was a question on a test, how would you answer it?"

"You're exasperating sometimes, you know that? Okay, SWAK; Spirit; remain calm. Knowledge; I have no idea what to do. Wisdom; don't paddle until I know which way to go. Action; hope someone comes by. Good luck with that. Toward sundown, maybe the western horizon will turn pink or red and I can paddle toward it. Paddle like crazy, that's for sure. Wait a minute; I did see a boat out there!"

The fishing boat skipper reached for his binoculars and double checked. His four clients, pleased with their catch, were enjoying their liquid refreshments, happy to be on their way home. Until the yellow kayak came into view he'd been looking forward to docking early. Pressing 'Talk' on the intercom he said, "Folks, were going to take a little detour. There's a kayaker clear out here. It's a lake kayak but they're waving their paddle in the air. I need to check it out."

When the fishing boat turned toward her Suzanne gratefully lowered the long, double ended paddle and slumped in the seat, rubbing her aching arms, and watching the boat approach. It was a typical charter vessel; spotless hull and gleaming hardware. Tips were more generous on immaculate boats.

The boat glided alongside, engines idling in reverse to stop it. "Are you okay?" asked a pudgy man sporting a White Sox baseball cap, sun-burnt ears, a half-empty beer bottle and a stubby cigar.

"Thanks for coming over. I need directions. I stopped to rest and dozed off. The sun has gone under and I don't have a compass or GPS. Which way is the shore?"

The man chuckled, "I'll have to ask the skipper, honey. We're on our way in and I'm not totally with it either. Here he comes now."

"Maybe! What are you doing clear out here?"

21

Oh, no! It's Dare, just my luck. "Hello, what do you mean clear out here? I'm just off shore but I can't tell where it is."

"I heard you say you 'dozed off'. You must have had a good nap. You are now about five miles off shore and about four miles north of Big Pine Harbor. You'd have to go some to get back before dark. I can take you in. I haven't got room for your kayak on deck, but you could come onboard, and we'll tow the kayak. Or, if you'd rather, I could tow you in the kayak, but the wake would make it pretty uncomfortable. Either way, I could put you off near your place."

"I don't know; which direction is Big Pine Harbor?"

"If you want to try paddling I'll loan you a compass. West-southwest should get you there. The wind got you here so paddling into it should get you close. Do you do much kayaking?"

"Not much. I guess I'd better come on board. Toss me the tow rope, I'll tie it on."

"If you don't mind I'll tie it on myself – with a secret sailor knot." Smirking, Dare vaulted over the side, splashing her with chilly water. Surfacing, he secured the rope and offered, "There's a ladder on the stern. I'll tow you around there."

"I'm sorry to bother all of you," Suzanne said, as she found her footing on the deck. "This is pretty embarrassing, I don't know if my Dad will lecture me or laugh at me."

"Probably both if he's anything like mine," said Dare. "It'll be chilly out here when we're underway. It's warmer in the wheelhouse if you'd like to come up; better view, too."

Deciding Dare would be better company than four rowdy middle-aged fishermen; she followed him to the wheelhouse thinking, *at least he stopped.*

"You're right Dare; the view up here is great; very different than from the kayak. You're very kind to do this. I don't know how I can thank you; I was in a real fix."

"No problem, Maybe. You might tell me your real name. And you could forgive me for whatever I've done to get off on the wrong foot with you."

"Do you bill all your clients so quickly?"

"Oh, you have it good," Dare replied with an easy smile, "Everyone else has to pay in advance."

"So, you're generous as well as kind," she said, sliding into a chair, "I guess I'd better pay up. My name is Suzanne and I kind of like to keep to myself. Do you take people out every day?"

"If I can; no fishermen, no pay. These guys have a nice catch and they'll have a good story to tell about rescuing a beautiful damsel in distress. I might get a good tip."

"I'll expect a commission."

"It's a deal. There's the Big Pine Harbor boardwalk. Are you north or south of it?"

"Just drop me off-shore from the boardwalk. I'll paddle on from there. Mom will be scared if she sees me being towed in."

Making her way to the stern as the boat stopped, Susan said, "I'm sorry about the detour guys. Thanks for your patience."

There was a chorus of "No problem," "Our pleasure," and "Anytime." Dare came from the wheelhouse and began pulling in, and neatly coiling, the tow line. As he worked he said, "You guys should see the unusual rock she found the other day. I've never seen anything like it. Do you have it with you, Suzanne? Could you show it to them?"

"Sorry, not today, Dare. How do I untie your secret sailor knot?" she asked, climbing down the stern ladder.

"Just pull on the free end." She did, carefully slid into the kayak and took the paddle from Dare.

Pushing off, she waved, calling out, "Thanks again guys." As the fishermen cheered her on, she paddled toward shore without looking back.

"Maybe we'll run into each other again," called Dare

"Maybe," she called over her shoulder. Home was in sight.

Dare went back to the wheelhouse and started the boat toward home with a little more throttle than necessary. One of the fishermen called out, "Hey Skipper, that was some catch. Too bad she got away," and Dare thought, *She is amazing, but she hasn't got away yet.*

22

Suzanne dragged the kayak across the cold sand, slid it under the deck, and placed the paddle next to it. Shadows covered the deck as she crossed and opened the door calling, "Mom? Dad? Anyone home?" Silence.

Entering, she jumped as she heard, "Nobody here but us chickens."

"Geez, Hugh, you scared me. So, you know all the colloquialisms, too? Do you know where that came from? It's an old joke. It's what the chicken thief said when the farmer hearing a commotion in his hen house one night, hollered, "Who's there?""

"That's pretty good. I only studied the language; I didn't research all the sources. It looks like your adventure is our secret."

"Let's keep it that way. I wonder where Mom and Dad are. Oh, there's a message on the phone."

"Hi Suzanne, you must be on the beach or something. Dad and I won't be home until late. Out of town friends called him at school and we're going to dinner with them. We'll see you this evening."

"I'm starving, Hugh. Refrigerator, here I come."

Between bites Suzanne said, "Thanks for your help this afternoon. If I'd panicked that boat might have gone right on by. The cover of *The Hitchhiker's Guide to the Galaxy* says, 'DON'T PANIC', and the Bible always says, 'Do not be afraid'. I never appreciated how important that is.

"Like when I was so scared last night, Hugh. Now I realize I didn't need to be afraid. I don't need to be afraid of God. Infinite knowledge means God understands my abilities and why I do what I do. And an infinitely right spirit means God wants only good things for me, like Mom and Dad do. I'm sad Mom doesn't understand all this. I can't imagine the pain it must cause God to see how I hurt myself and others when I screw up, even if it's by accident or because I don't know how to do any better. It must be hard being God."

"It's a big job."

"Hugh, how much family do you have in your time?"

"I'm an only child of only children. Few families have more than one or two children. My parents died three of our years ago when a small meteorite punctured their living quarters causing it to explosively lose air pressure."

"I'm sorry, Hugh. Does that kind of thing happen often?"

"It's actually quite rare. I miss them, but it happened quickly, and they didn't suffer. I probably wouldn't be here if it hadn't happened."

Suzanne sat silently, arms folded, looking out the window at nothing in particular. After a while she said, "They were good people, weren't they?"

"Yes, I and many others loved and admired them."

"I wonder why bad things happen to good people, Hugh. It doesn't seem fair."

"Who do you suppose decides what should happen to people, Suzanne?"

"God, I guess."

"And what do we know about God, Suzanne?"

"Ohh. God is perfect, infinite Love and wants only the best for everyone," clamping her hands on her temples she continued, "So does that mean every bad thing is actually good? That bites. It might be true sometimes, but it can't be always. It just can't."

"So, what else could cause bad things?"

"Well, people. People cause bad things because they don't make good decisions, or they have a bad attitude. Or they don't know what they're doing." Suzanne stood quickly and began pacing around the room. "Omigosh, bad things happen because it's impossible for people to Love perfectly, that's all! Our physical bodies and minds don't have infinite capabilities. It's not God's fault. It makes God sad. I need to write this down, Hugh."

Pulling the pad from her bag and sitting down she paused. "I wonder why God didn't just make people perfect in the first place. Then there wouldn't be any bad things. Well, except like what happened to your parents. But if they were infinitely wise with infinite knowledge I guess they would have known a meteorite would strike in that spot.

Um, wait a minute, Hugh. You had me convinced 'nothing happens until someone cares,' and 'Love is all there is,' but I'm not so sure. Those can be useful statements, but I don't think they're absolutely true. I'll agree if we're talking about people getting along with each other, but what about stuff? Stuff like houses and meteorites and cars and books; and trees and oceans and stars? Those aren't Love; they don't have spirit or knowledge or wisdom.

It's getting really dark in here, Hugh." Turning on a lamp, Suzanne heard car doors in the garage and the kitchen door opened.

23

"Hi Suzanne, did you have a good day? We had a wonderful visit with the Johanssons. Do you remember them? They lived four doors down when you were little. They moved to St. Paul when you were in Kindergarten. They were sorry they missed you."

"Hi Mom, Dad. I've been writing since I got back from kayaking. You guys were due for a night out together, but I don't remember the Johanssons. I'm about finished writing, then I'm headed for bed."

"We're turning in, too. See you in the morning."

"Good night."

Starting up the stairs Suzanne asked Hugh, "Now, can you explain about 'stuff'?"

"I think you already know the answer."

"Aren't you the clever one! Are you ever going to just answer a simple question?"

"You're right, it is a simple question, Suzanne. Think about it. Like, where do books come from?"

"You make me crazy. Books come from people who have an idea and write it down to share with other people. Satisfied?"

"Almost."

"What do you mean 'almost'? That's it, Hugh. It's obvious. People write books because they want to. Because they . . . ohhh, I get it, they care, someone cares. Books are products of Love. Same for houses and cars and other stuff. But that still doesn't explain meteorites and trees and oceans and stars. This makes my head hurt. I'll think about it later."

"It'll come to you, maybe tomorrow."

"Yeah, me and Scarlett O'Hara. Good night, Hugh."

Gusty wind knocked and rattled at the eaves and white capped waves bellowed onto the sandy beach as Suzanne fought her covers, dreaming of galaxies exploding into life and imploding back into darkness.

* * * * * * *

The quiet, and the warm glow of impending sunrise, woke her. Groggily straightening the blankets over herself she thought, *What a night! That was weird. I wonder if these strange nights have anything to do with Hugh. I wonder if he's really in the rock or if he's just my mind playing tricks on me. Oh well, he does make life interesting.*

Half-awake she idly mused; *Books and cars and houses and "things" are the products of people's Love. Meteorites and trees and oceans and stars are so big they're nearly infinite. They can't be the product of Love.*

"Excuse me for interrupting, Suzanne, but are you sure?"

"I thought you said you couldn't hear me unless I spoke to you."

"I did say that. I also said you sometimes speak to me without knowing it, like now."

"Well, thank you for paying attention, Mr. Hugh."

"You're welcome, Miss Suzanne. Now, are you sure those things can't be the product of Love?"

"Yes, they're too big. It would have to be someone infinite."

"Like?"

"Like infinite Love . . . Ohhh. Yeah, that works. Perfect infinite love would have the know-how and the power and everything to do the job. You're right, I already knew the answer ... or at least the words to the answer – it's God," she smiled.

"Okay, Suzanne, we know where the materials come from for cars and houses and books. Where do you suppose the materials came from for meteorites and trees and oceans and stars?"

"Ha, that's not so hard. They came from the big bang."

"Ah, yes, and the material for the big bang came from where?"

24

"Suzanne, would you like breakfast before I put things away?"

"Sure, Mom. I'll be right down."

* * * * * * *

"That was delicious, Mom. I'll take care of the dishes. Enjoy yourself."

"Thanks, dear. Janet Evanovich and I will be out on the deck."

Filling the sink, she said, "Hugh, I've been thinking about that big bang question. It's hard, but since there wasn't anything else before the big bang, I guess the materials would have to have been part of God. Oh! That means the universe is made of Love! Cool stuff! I'm made of Love, too! I'm made of God! Not infinite, so I can't be perfect, but the same stuff. I'm made of stardust and stardust is made of God-stuff. Awesome! Guess that explains the bit about being made in God's image. And I thought those Sunday school stories were, like, fables."

"There's truth everywhere, Suzanne; more some places than others."

"That doesn't sound right but I'll think about it later; right now, I'm wondering about some of the other God stuff I was told at Sunday school. Like, if God made us so it's impossible for us to always do the right thing, why did Jesus have to die so God would forgive us for our screw-ups?"

Washing her favorite cup, Suzanne was reminded of the Easter it was given to her. She was five years old and it had rained on her new Easter dress; but the gift of a 'grown-up' cup decorated with her favorite daisies and filled with chocolate eggs made up for everything.

The cup slipped from her wet hands. Striking the floor, the handle shattered, and the cup rolled under the kitchen table.

"Rats! I need a broom. I've screwed up again!"

"Again, Suzanne?"

"That was my favorite cup, Hugh. I guess that's what I deserve for being so clumsy."

"Are you listening to yourself? Do you really believe that?"

"Believe what?"

"That you are being punished for being clumsy?"

"Since you put it that way, Hugh, I guess the broken handle isn't punishment, it's just the result of not being perfect. But I still feel guilty, I can't help it. Look at all those tiny pieces, there's no way it can be glued together. Out they go."

"There's that 'guilty' word again. I wonder why it keeps coming up?"

"I don't know. Why do you always ask questions, Hugh? Everybody feels guilty when they do something stupid or bad; it's normal."

"How's that working for you?"

"That's unkind. It's not working well at all. I'm angry and sad and I feel terrible."

"Would it help if I tell you it's my fault? If I take the blame?"

"You broke my cup? Now I'm angry with you!"

"Please don't throw me in the trash, too, Suzanne.

"Are you going to keep the unbroken part of the cup? Do you feel better now?"

"I feel a little bit better. I'm not mad at myself anymore, and yes, I am going to save the cup. Why did you do that, Hugh? I loved this cup. And no, I won't throw you away."

"Thank you. Actually, I didn't break the cup, but I may have distracted you. You were wondering why Jesus had to die so God would forgive us for our screw-ups. We may have just uncovered some clues. Let's see where they take us."

"It's confusing, Hugh. The mind and body God gave us limit what we can know and do, and God loves us, so why does God make Jesus take the blame for our shortcomings and mistakes?"

"Did you feel better about yourself, freer, when I said the cup was my fault?"

"Sure, it took a real load of guilt off."

"Earlier you said God understands you and wants only the best for you. Right, Suzanne?"

"Right."

"Then, how would you explain Jesus?"

"Well, first of all, I know God isn't looking to punish anyone for being what 'He' made us to be, even though 'She' might feel really sorry for us sometimes.

"You know, 'He' and 'She' don't fit God very well.

"Anyway, maybe Jesus, besides teaching us about Love, wanted to take away the blame and punishment we think we deserve when we make mistakes or do bad things. When that is out of the way we can come to know God's Love more like Jesus did, and our life will be much better. This is giving me chills. It's so big."

"You're getting good at this, Suzanne. I'm sorry about your cup."

"All that from a broken cup." *Sigh*, "What am I going to do with all this, Hugh?"

25

"I can still use the cup. Maybe Dad can show me how to smooth the sharp edges where the handle broke off. It might still feel good in my hand on a chilly day.

"Hugh, what do you want me to do? You said you needed my help."

"What would you like to do, Suzanne?"

"You are incorrigible! I asked first."

"Yes, you did, but you will be best at something you really want to do. So, what do you really want to do?"

"I would really like to share what I've learned, but I don't know how. I don't know enough."

"You will never know enough, Suzanne. You can always learn more, but you will always know enough to do something."

"Suzanne," sang her mother, "would you be a dear and bring me a glass of iced tea? This Janet Evanovich page turner has me glued to my chair. You may want to join me, it's beautiful out here."

"Sure, I'll make two and be right out."

Putting ice cubes and sun tea in insulated glasses, Suzanne said, "Hugh, I've been thinking; let's talk silently on the deck about this."

"Deal! Is that the way to say it?"

Elbowing the screen door open and stepping onto the sunny warm deck boards, Suzanne said, "Mom, I'll set your tea here beside you since your hands are busy turning pages. I'm going to just sit in this rocker and watch the lake a while."

"Thank you, dear."

"You're welcome."

She silently said, "That's good, Hugh. Do you have such sayings at home? Did you speak English?"

"When our people left Earth most spoke English, but our language has evolved into something unique to our planet. Like yours, it's always changing."

"Some time, I'd like to learn some of it, Hugh."

Ice cubes rattled as she sipped the chilly tea and thought, "You know, I've been thinking; We were talking about sharing what I've learned. I guess I could begin by just 'being' Love to the best of my ability and see where it goes."

"You might be surprised, Suzanne; the fabric of life is full of them. Everyone connects to different existing threads, spins unique threads of their own and connects them in unique ways, creating this beautiful fabric. You never know how far away a thread originated and you never know how far your threads will extend. That makes every individual unique – and important to more than the present."

"I like that image, Hugh," she said with a sigh.

"School starts soon. I'm going to start organizing all the things I've written about Love. I'll add to it as we go along."

Sipping tea, watching small sailboats skim the lake, she added, "You are coming along, aren't you?"

"I'm right here."

✎ The Beginning ✎

AFTER WORD

Hugh, Dare, and her family continued to be part of Suzanne's life. Good times or difficult, she Loved it all, expanding her Knowledge, honing her Spirit, growing in Wisdom, and writing in her notebook.

She shared Love, inspiring many people, and taught Love to many people and Artificial Intelligence computer programs.

You can imagine how her relationships and observations might have led to her later notes. If you would like to write an episode (500 words or less) and share it with the author, it may become part of a future anthology.

Barry Gulliver
LILT Publishing LLC
220 So. Lakeview
Sturgis, MI 49091

Notes

NOTEBOOK OF

Suzanne B.

Dedicated to my friend, Hugh

love
is LOVE.
All is LOVE.
Their all is LOVE.
LOVE is all there is.
LOVE is all there.
LOVE is all.
LOVE is.
LOVE.

DEAR READER,

This notebook began when I met Hugh on a sunny beach one brisk summer morning. It is a collection of discoveries recorded over the years as I explored ramifications of the Love Paradigm. I hope you will find them as helpful as I have.

Most entries are brief rather than in-depth. I find each a catalyst for further thoughtful exploration, building on previous knowledge and experience.

There are no supporting references or footnotes, and a reader would be derelict to accept any of it without critical thought. I fully expect every reader's life experience will cast different lights on LOVE and call to mind different supporting references.

You may find, written at different times, variations on the same subject. That is as it should be. I find LOVE to be infinitely varied and infinitely interconnected, without beginning or end.

If an open and inquiring mind, and postponing conclusions, are not part of your present paradigm, please pretend for a while. Whatever your final conclusions, I hope they will be better illuminated and better understood than before.

Do turn down corners of pages, write thoughts and observations on the pages. Leave tracks; you will enjoy, as I do, meeting your former self when returning.

A journey of exploration sometimes
reminds one why they appreciate their home,
and sometimes leads to a new home.

Aristotle, in "Metaphysics," said,
"No one is able to attain the truth adequately,
while on the other hand we do not collectively fail; but
each one says something true about the nature of things,
and while, individually, we contribute little or nothing to
the truth, by all of us together, a considerable amount is
amassed."

This notebook is shared in that spirit.

Suzanne

INTRODUCTION

It is not uncommon to miss what is right in front of us because we believe we already "know" everything about it. Love is like that. We are surrounded by it, we are "swimming" in it, but we only see as much of it as we expect to. We often tend to see only the "nice" part. People being nice to us and us being nice to other people are wonderful aspects of Love but they only hint at the full dimensions of Love.

We often speak of love and generally regard it as a good thing, especially in the sense of "Love thy neighbor," but think about it. What do we really mean by "love?"

Is Love our feelings – for a favorite food, type of weather, possession, performer, or TV show? Is it romantic love for another person? Is it the relationship we have with a treasured pet? Is it concern for friends or neighbors? This could go on and on; we use the word "love" so many ways.

I use capital "L" LOVE when referring to the over-arching LOVE I have come to know.

BIG WORDS

Love, Happiness, Good, Bad, Faith, Sin, Guilt.

Big words. Foundational words.

The biggest, most important words in every language are typically the least defined. Everyone grows up "just knowing" what they mean. To define or explain them is most often regarded as silly, senseless, or even heretical.

Perhaps this is because they are such basic facts of life that they define all others, making it impossible to fully explain them. Perhaps it is because they touch areas conventional language can't adequately describe.

However, if the foundation of anything is not clearly understood, it is impossible to fully comprehend the construction, characteristics, use and capabilities of that which rests upon it.

There is work to do.

KEY DEFINITIONS

(Used in this notebook.)

love (verb, small "l") Warm, caring feelings and actions directed towards a person, object or creature.

sin (verb, small "s") Any behavior, attitude, or action which falls short of perfection, thus spoiling something good.

Sin (noun, capital "S") The origin of sin. The fact of the imperfection and imperfectability of everything in this world. (Traditionally: The knowledge or idea of good and evil, right and wrong. This feeds a persistent belief "good" will be rewarded and anything "not good" will, and must, be punished.)

God Infinite, all-encompassing Love, called by many names; Jehovah, Yahweh, Allah, Brahman, the Tao, the Great Spirit, etc.

NOTE: *How shall I refer to God here? It is inaccurate to refer to God as an entity in speech or in writing such as this. There is a long tradition of "Him" and "His", and a newer practice of "Him/Her" and "His/Hers" but none are remotely descriptive of God who is infinitely beyond the narrow constraints of human bodies, thought, and language. So, even though it may sometimes trip the tongue or eye, God shall simply be referred to as "God" and the possessive form used shall be "God's". (Try to keep in mind; God is nothing less than infinite and perfect Love, and there is nothing else. More on that later)*

Love   (noun, verb, capital "L")   What I have learned with Hugh's help. It is comprehensive, but simple. Read on, then create your own definition.

The many facets of Love have long been known, admired, and examined, but not always in relationship to one another; as a complete gem. Even if each element, or facet, of this discussion may be familiar to you, remain alert, for as every diamond cutter knows, great beauty arises not from individual facets, but from their relationships and interactions with each other.

ATTRIBUTES OF Love

On following pages, I have listed some attributes of Love. When adding to these, please use positive terms only – for example, "generous" rather than "not selfish" or "not stingy". This may be difficult at first, since negative terms often come more quickly to mind than positive words; but fight the good fight, negatives will be addressed later.

Attributes are divided into four sections – Spirit (for items of spirit, conscience, and attitude), Knowledge, Wisdom, and Action, it must be understood these are arbitrary divisions of a cohesive whole and all four parts exist and operate simultaneously, seamlessly and harmoniously.

Again, remember, a capital "L" is used to differentiate all-encompassing Love from its subsets, "love" and "loving". Understanding and remembering that Love does not always involve "liking" is difficult, but critically important.

Love SPIRIT

Love Spirit is a frame of mind, motivation, mindset, attitude, state of mind, or state of being. It is:

open minded	compassion	selfless	cool
empathy	courage	perseverance	joy
confidence	tranquility	humility	kindness
tolerance	resilience	peace	strength
forgiveness	sensitivity	respect	modesty
generosity	nurturing	patience	guilt free
honesty (with self & others)		rejoicing in the truth	
accepting (of self & others)		willingness to learn	
celebration			

Add yours . . .

Love KNOWLEDGE

Love Knowledge is all information available to us at the moment. It is:

concern	experiment	anticipation	
curiosity	sensitive	listening	alert
interest	inquiry	aware	taste
reading	seeing	memory	smell
happiness	anger	seeking	fear
sadness	pleasure	intuition	anxiety
disappointment		gut feelings	

Add your own . . .

KNOWLEDGE MATTERS

A motorcyclist riding through the mountains early on a frosty fall morning became chilled by wind blowing through the zipper of his jacket. He stopped, reversed the jacket so it zipped up the back, and rode on up the mountain.

A few miles later, he lost control on a frost covered curve, hurtled into the trees and fell unconscious at the base of a huge pine tree. An oncoming motorist saw the accident, stopped, sent another motorist to get an ambulance, and rushed down the mountain to help. The motorist quickly checked the cyclist and began to help as well as he could.

As the ambulance attendants came into the trees they asked the condition of the cyclist. "I'm afraid it's too late." said the motorist, "He was breathing when I got to him, but he died just as I got his head turned around right."

Love WISDOM

Love Wisdom is the analytical and creative powers we bring to a situation. Wisdom:

knows itself	cares	creates
understands	analyzes	considers all knowledge
enjoys	is fair	solves problems
thorough	seeks truth	considers all options
looks ahead	even-handed	makes decisions
discerns	finds basic objective/purpose	
gut feelings	finds root cause/problem/issue	

Add your own....

Wisdom is modest and recognizes it is not omnipotent.
Wisdom recognizes it does not possess Truth (capital T),
only what it currently knows to be true (small t).

Kevin Gulliver

Love ACTION

Love Action is the physical effect we are able to apply or cause. It is:

appropriate	generous	fun	patient
persistent	thorough	kind	helpful
skillful	involved	timely	unselfish
courageous	resilient	nurturing	effective
celebrates			

Add your own....

A man must sit with his mouth open a long time
before a roast duck will fly into it.

Ancient Oriental proverb

NAMES WE GIVE EXTREMES

Any abundance, or deficiency, of one or more aspects of Love is generally named and often mistakenly regarded as a distinct personal characteristic, implying it is entirely separate from its "opposite"

In actuality, only "good" characteristics exist. "Bad", or opposite, characteristics are simply deficiencies, or lesser degrees, of the "good". Examples from the physical world are heat and cold, which seem very different and have many names but actually are only greater or lesser degrees of heat. Other examples are light and darkness, pressure and vacuum, and wet and dry.

Different gradations of Love have different names depending on the "level" or "quality" of Love present, but all are simply Love's variations. A few examples are listed below. A dashed line means any level could be present, "avg." means average.

ACTION	KNOWLEDGE	WISDOM	RIGHT SPIRIT	NAME
----	low	----	----	Ignorant
avg.	avg.	avg.	high	Kind
high	avg.	low	----	Careless
----	----	low	----	Stupid
avg.	avg.	avg.	avg.	Nice
low	----	----	----	Lazy
----	----	----	low	Wicked
high	high	high	low	Evil
----	high	high	avg.	Wise
high	high	high	high	Divine

Understanding the make-up of a characteristic
makes it possible to respond appropriately.

DEGREES OF Love

The concept of "gradations or degrees of Love" is important in understanding and dealing with issues of education, personal development, and dealing with difficult people and situations.

For one thing, it means "bad" or "evil," as such, cannot be fought, driven out, or conquered because it has no form or existence. It is only a lack of something positive.

Only Love is real and substantial. Just as darkness cannot be destroyed or driven out, only displaced by light, "bad" or "evil" can only be diminished by increasing the positive characteristics of Love.

WHAT ABOUT EVIL?

Evil lives, and sometimes briefly thrives, but in the end collapses in upon itself.

Evil is usually perceived as separate from, opposite of, and opposed to, Love. This is not true. The Love Paradigm (more on that later, pg. 115) reveals Evil for what it is, grossly deformed and defective Love. Clearly seeing Evil for what it is greatly reduces its power.

Evil is the name we use for very poor-quality Right Spirit combined with high levels of Knowledge, Power and Wisdom. Evil is solely devoted to caring about itself. The near absence of Right Spirit and the inability to understand it in others are Evil's fatal flaws.

The primary result of Evil persons or powers is to diminish, obscure, or displace high quality Love. The most insidious, subversive work of Evil is to encourage opposition to itself, thus increasing its effect by diverting energy and attention from expanding and strengthening quality Love. Raging against the darkness of Evil, consumes far more energy and resources than lighting a candle, or a hundred candles of Love.

Although Evil cannot be destroyed, or even subdued by battle, it can be disabled and marginalized. It can be Loved nearly to death.

When faced with Evil, remember; Love is Right Spirit, Wisdom, Knowledge, and Action, well balanced and complete. Evil is defective in Spirit, which limits the effectiveness of its Knowledge, Wisdom and Action. "Love your enemy" is essential. Know everything possible about the Evil, consider that knowledge carefully and take Loving action to minimize its effects and frustrate its efforts. Eventually Evil will defeat itself.

TRUTH (1)

Truth is absolutely essential to quality Love. It is elusive, but without a steadfast effort to find, see, hear, accept, and tell the truth, everything we are and do rests on shifting sand.

There are many faces to the truth. Is the truth of a cattail plant the marvelous exploding hot dog on a stick and elegant green spears of foliage? Or is it the edible bud, or the bulb that removes toxic materials from the environment? Or is it something else? Or is it all those things and even more we do not yet know?

What is the truth of a statement? The words? Which interpretation? Nuances of delivery? The speaker's intention? The perception of the hearer?

What is the truth of an action? The preparation? The quality of implementation? The immediate effect? The long-term effect? The motivation? The intent? An observer's perception?

We can never know the whole truth. We can come closer by learning from the perceptions of those with different eyes and hearts.

Just as there are many faces to the truth, there are many ways to tell the truth. Telling the truth is more than simply stating facts. Love tells truth in helpful ways. It considers both speaker's and hearer's spirit, knowledge, and experience. It tells truth in ways the hearer can understand and use to grow Love in themselves and the world.

TRUTH (2)

Love treasures the truth,
even when it hurts,

Love discerns the truth,
Love hears the truth,
Love accepts the truth,

Love tells the truth,
with kindness.

Love is the truth.

Love IS

Love is not just something nice to do,
or something we should do.
It is not the most wonderful thing we can fall into

Love is life.
Love is all there is to life.
If we live, we Love – sometimes very well,
sometimes poorly,
but we only Love.

We have no choice,
except how well we Love.

Love IS ALL

Look again at the lists of Love attributes. (pg. 100-105) Consider this question, "Is there anything in the entire world that is not Love or the result of Love?"

There is nothing.

Everything and everyone springs from the same root, infinite perfect Love. Everything and everyone is made of the same stuff and contributes to the growth of Love in the world. Every thing and every one has both limitations and potential for growth in Love. By knowing this, we can interact more harmoniously with the rest of the world; participating, aiding and growing Love rather than only struggling to ward off and battle the deficiencies and discomforts of life.

This idea everything is Love or the product of Love, certainly affects the way one thinks about the world, one's neighbors, and one's self!

It takes practice to begin seeing the world this way. There is a natural tendency to slip back into believing only in Good & Bad, Reward and Punishment, and the warm, fuzzy, limited version of (small "l") love which lead to confusion and unsatisfactory results. Neither life nor this book will make much sense unless using large "L" Love.

Practice thinking Spirit, Wisdom, Action, Knowledge (SWAK).

Practice. Practice. Practice.

You will appreciate the results.

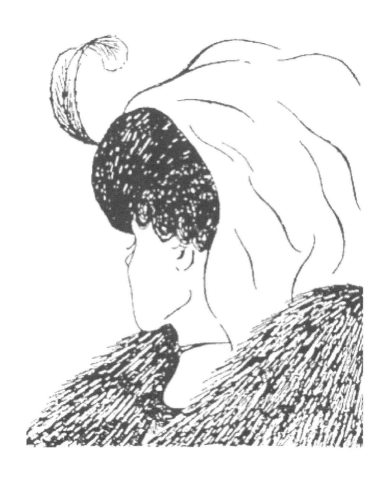

What do you see?

An old woman? A young woman?

Look again.

The LOVE Paradigm

The LOVE paradigm makes sense
of a confusing world.
It empowers us to be more than we are,
and inspires us to engage the world
in positive and rewarding ways.

PARADIGMS

The parents of seven-year-old twins became concerned the first was unnaturally pessimistic and the second was extraordinarily optimistic. Hoping to help them view the world more realistically, the parents selected special birthday gifts for them.

When the children entered the room for their birthday party, a beautiful red bicycle awaited the first child who chattered about its beauty and how much fun it would be, then asked to go out for a ride. The parents' pleasure was short lived. The child began reciting all the terrible things that might happen to a child on a bicycle and decided it should be stored in the garage until later.

The second child noticed a gift box larger than himself, tore away the ribbons and bows, opened it, and discovered it empty except for several horse droppings in the bottom. Confused for a moment the child quickly recovered and excitedly said, "I got a pony! I got a pony! He's gone now, but he'll be right back!"

A paradigm is, quite simply, a model or pattern. In contemporary usage, "paradigm" usually refers to "*a pattern of thought which affects the way facts and events are interpreted and utilized.*" A useful paradigm is a foundation and shortcut, which makes it possible for a person to act without figuring out everything from the beginning each time a decision must be made.

These deeply rooted frameworks of beliefs, information, assumptions, and thought patterns, determine how an individual sees, interprets, and interacts with the world.

They are small things, the bits of observations, lessons and conclusions that combine to form the paradigm that guides us, but their effects are profound and far-reaching. They determine who we are, who we will become and whom we will welcome into our lives. Yet, although huge in their effect, they are most often invisible to us.

Formed "behind the scenes", without conscious choice, and operating invisibly at the most fundamental level, a paradigm's "output" is often held to be "common sense" or "obvious", and beyond argument, analysis or discussion.

While preparing breakfast, a college freshman mentioned that buttered toast always falls butter-side down. As a second freshman argued it would be a 50-50 chance, the first freshman's toast slipped and fell to the floor – landing butter-side up. Stunned, the first freshman hesitated then said, "Oh, I see now, I buttered the wrong side of the toast!"

Besides buttered toast, other paradigms outgrown by most people are: "Bad weather is a sign the gods are angry," "The universe revolves around the Earth," and "Some races are born superior to other races." At one time each of these paradigms seemed beyond doubt and was regarded as useful but was replaced as new experiences and information became available.

It often takes a major emotional event or great courage and effort to change a paradigm because anything different seems, at first, "unnatural" and uncomfortable. In the case of LOVE, the change is well worth the effort.

THE GOOD/BAD -
REWARD/PUNISHMENT PARADIGM
(G/B-R/P)

Nature and nurture have led us astray. They have combined to teach us a bipolar, paradoxical paradigm of good and bad, reward and punishment. The teaching is so subtle and pervasive we accept this misleading paradigm, not just as an unquestionable fact of life but often as life itself.

Some will protest, "But life *is* good and bad, it operates by rewards and punishments!" They speak their paradigm. They have mistaken natural consequences for punishments and rewards.

Believing life to be a series of "good" or "bad" episodes creates the immediate problem of deciding in which category an episode belongs. It is impossible. For example, the person who wins a huge sum of money (good) then ruins their life in reckless dissipation and dies broken (bad); or the person whose life of reckless dissipation (bad) brings them to the edge of a despair that changes their life and they go on to do great works (good). Or the child of impoverished, neglectful, or even hurtful, parents (bad) who grows up resolved to be better than that – and succeeds (good). It is impossible to draw a clear and consistent line between "good" and "bad". What seems to be true at one point in time often turns out differently. Attempting such determinations leads only to complexity, confusion and frustration.

The pride, fear and guilt of a G/B-R/P paradigm complicate our relationships with others and with ourselves. Because it is constantly at war with itself and the world, the G/B-R/P paradigm prevents us from realistically comprehending the universe we live in, and from fully achieving our potential.

Be alert, the G/B-R/P paradigm is pervasive. Even though every great religious and philosophical teacher has attempted to displace the G/B-R/P paradigm, as time has passed, their teachings have been widely trimmed or stretched to fit the Procrustean bed of the very paradigm they intended to replace.

Procrustes, an innkeeper in Greek mythology, guaranteed his beds would perfectly fit any traveler – and they did – after the unfortunate sojourner was stretched or shortened!

THE Love PARADIGM

Most everyone believes LOVE is good. Although everyone has experience and knowledge of LOVE, few put the pieces together to entirely realize what LOVE is. LOVE consists of knowledge, a right spirit, wisdom and, of course, appropriate action.

Deficiency in one or more of those means trouble and excellence means positive results; not as punishment or rewards dispensed from somewhere, but as results natural as a finger burnt in a candle flame.

Understanding the world as a great mish-mash of LOVE in varying degrees of excellence (the LOVE paradigm) clearly reveals the wholeness and inter-relatedness of the world and everything in it. There are no longer opposing factions and forces to balance or reconcile, nor rewards and punishments to seek or fear. There are only opportunities for growth, understanding and improvement.

The LOVE paradigm is a coherent and robust paradigm. It is a most helpful way of understanding and using all we know. The LOVE paradigm illuminates life's meaning and purpose, harmony and wholeness, sweetness, and strength. It nurtures the positive roots of the world. The LOVE paradigm dramatically alters our perception of the world, and the effectiveness of our interaction with it.

It is important.

Love

To grasp the paradigm, we must understand LOVE. LOVE is the E=MC^2 of human life, very simple in concept yet pervasive and comprehensive in its application. Those with courage or curiosity to explore LOVE will find life, beneath the misunderstandings and misinterpretations, is in fact, a continuum of LOVE rather than a series of disconnected rewards and punishments.

- LOVE makes sense.
- LOVE is harmonious.
- LOVE is strong.
- LOVE works.
- LOVE is all there is.
- The elements of LOVE are Spirit, Knowledge, Wisdom, and Action.
- God is perfect, infinite, LOVE.
- We are made of LOVE, although imperfect in diverse ways.
- We are part of God.
- Most things we name love are subsets of LOVE.
- The purpose of life is to nurture LOVE, in others and in our self.

A NOTE

I believe the LOVE paradigm meshes with, and makes better and more consistent sense of, the knowledge and wisdom of the ages than any paradigm currently in wide use.

Where the LOVE paradigm is the norm, under whatever name, there is harmony and productivity. Where the LOVE paradigm is on the sidelines, there is fear, confusion and continuing cycles of violence. What peace and progress we now enjoy is due to many people practicing the LOVE paradigm to some degree.

The LOVE paradigm is certainly not the last word in understanding our lives. There is much we do not know about things beyond our senses and our high-tech sensors. New discoveries will reveal new frontiers. However, the LOVE paradigm provides a strong foundation for exploring, and thriving on, those new frontiers.

I encourage you to test the paradigm, as I continue to do. Put it on, wear it a while, try it out, feel it, poke at it, question it, see how it holds up.

It will not always be easy, but it will be very rewarding.

Suzanne

IT IS OLD

The Love paradigm is actually very old; It lies at the very roots of the universe and, thus, virtually every lasting religious belief and philosophical system. (Often, the Love root has sprouted in a form that only partially reveals it. Sometimes the true character of Love is obscured or distorted by accumulated minutiae of ritual or doctrine.)

It is not so much that all groups teach the paradigm, as it is that all have common roots in LOVE, and their practices, beliefs and teachings originated in LOVE.

Apparent differences arise because of emphasis on different aspects and manifestations of Love. The Love paradigm illuminates their common origin, enriching every group by giving them more direct access to their roots.

SEALED WITH A KISS

It takes time, attention and effort to change a paradigm. Work to do Love and eventually become Love in all your thoughts and actions.

If you find it difficult to remember the "elements" of Love as you are dealing with a situation, remember SWAK.

SWAK was originally a "secret" romantic message applied to the flap of a "snail-mail" envelope, indicating it had been Sealed With A Kiss.

It can also be used to remind you of the four elements of LOVE:

Spirit

Wisdom

Action

Knowledge

Stick with the project; you will be pleased with the results.

SWAK

Love IS NOT OPTIONAL

LOVE is not optional.

It is not a choice.

It is impossible to not LOVE.

The only choice we have,

is to LOVE poorly,

or to LOVE well.

It is a curious thing.

LITTLE THINKERS

The following brief entries are included with hope some will set off productive chains of thought, provide enlightenment, or maybe even a good chuckle.

Write all over the pages, turn down corners. You will enjoy meeting yourself when you return.

Enjoy.

Suzanne

THE OPERATING SYSTEM

Love 1.0 is the Operating System
of the universe.

THE PURPOSE OF LIFE

The purpose of life is to nurture LOVE.

We are born as LOVE. We are Spirit, Action, Knowledge and Wisdom. There is nothing else. When we are born we have very limited strength in any of these, but we grow and learn. The stronger we grow; the more harmonious and pleasant life becomes. And, as we grow individually stronger, LOVE itself grows.

The limitations of this life give us the opportunity to learn LOVE. We see the confusion, frustration and pain of developing LOVE contrasted with the beauty, harmony and effectiveness of strong LOVE, and from the contrast, we get hints of the magnificence of perfect LOVE. We prepare to fully appreciate perfect LOVE, and to fully be LOVE when we shed the limitations of this world.

If our job is to nurture LOVE and to be LOVE, how does this affect our role as parents? as neighbors? as workers? as consumers? as citizens? as occupants of the Earth?

FEELING GOOD

If you don't feel good about what you are doing,
you are either doing the wrong thing,

or doing the thing wrong.

FORCE

A disagreement settled by force is not settled; it is only concealed, and often intensified.

Force is sometimes necessary to temporarily protect others or self, or to protect someone from them self; but force does not eliminate the problem that led to the need for intervention.

World War II did not change the "enemy's" minds and hearts. Years of thoughtful aid and reconstruction did that and made that part of the world a more peaceful place.

THE HIKERS

Two hungry hikers found their way obstructed by a large patch of briars.

Grumbling, the first hiker charged directly into them, determined to reach his destination. The briars tore his skin and clothing, frequently halting progress while he disentangled himself.

The second hiker, pausing at the edge of the briar patch to catch his breath, noticed plump, ripe berries on the branches and began to pick and eat those he could easily reach. Munching happily, he became aware of animal trails meandering throughout the briars. Carefully moving along them in the general direction of his journey, he continued to pluck and enjoy the sweet fruit and arrived, refreshed, at the other side just as his exhausted companion stumbled out.

Life is a briar patch.

Love IS WHAT?

Love is a term we use often and in many ways. We all agree it is a good thing, but often do not agree on what it is. That is because each of us is thinking of a different small part of a very large thing.

Rather like the four blind people, each touching a different part of an elephant and each attempting to convince the others an elephant is similar to either; 1. a rope (tail), 2. a large column (leg), 3. a very large snake (trunk), or 4. a great boulder (side). Each person's facts and experience were beyond question and each argued with absolute conviction, unable to understand how the others could cling so fiercely to such peculiar views.

Love is like that. It is a single huge thing with four "faces.". One face is a Right Spirit, or caring attitude, or peaceful state of mind. Another is Action, getting involved, helping, or doing. Another is Wisdom, to decide rightly what is best to do or not do. Another is possession of Knowledge, for fully informed decisions. If these things are strong, we say, "that is good." If one or more of these things are weak, we say "that is bad."

Love is . . . everything. Sometimes stronger, sometimes weaker, sometimes appearing to have one form and sometimes another. Love is all there is.

PATTERNS

It is the nature of living creatures

to discern apparent patterns,

and to use them to apparent benefit,

for self or others.

DUTY (1)

The concept of duty is troublesome. It is good to help our country, community, environment and other people. It is good for them and good for each of us. But "Duty" is a red herring. It draws us away from more important things and stunts our development.

No one speaks of their duty to do something they enjoy. "Duty" is a name most often given to something unpleasant, difficult or dangerous; Something we must do because someone, or our self, says we must – for our own good or the good of others.

Duty as an imposed obligation or command, deprives us of the creative act, and joy, of noticing a need and deciding, in LOVE, how and when to act. It shrivels the mind and spirit of the dutiful.

A Duty, pre-determined in a different time and place and blindly served in the present, cannot effectively deal with the intricacies of a present situation. And, there is always the age-old question, "Who should tell us what our duty is?" It has never been satisfactorily answered.

History has revealed patterns of actions tending to give "good" results, and actions to avoid because of their "bad" results. However, when these patterns become absolutes, in the form of Duties, both society and its individuals become inflexible, brittle, and unresponsive to the actual needs of the moment.

DUTY (2)

Duty "fulfilled" encourages unhealthy pride in our own actions rather than a more appropriate joy in the results of that action. Duty also creates a tendency to look down on those perceived to have neglected their Duty.

Duty unfulfilled generates scorn in others and guilt in one's self.

When Duty is chosen in Love, the Duty label can mislead us into a narrow understanding of what we are doing.

Quality Love creatively and productively responds to opportunities of the moment. Of course, quality Love will sometimes appear to be a "dutiful" response if the chosen action is identical to one dictated by Duty, but there is a huge difference in the effect on the person performing the action.

A person being quality Love grows in spirit, knowledge, wisdom, creativity and joy. A Dutiful person becomes susceptible to feelings of guilt for not performing as well as hoped, anger at their lack of freedom, or self-righteous pride for performing their Duty well.

While not always safe, easy or pleasant, quality Love enriches the entire being of everyone involved, as useful responses evolve for diverse situations.

Duty is simply doing; Love is being. Be quality Love.

WHAT IS GOOD?

Anything that grows LOVE is good.

There is no absolute measure.

Good is a milepost on the journey of LOVE.

AS NATURAL AS BREATHING

Love is as natural as breathing.

Most people love many things and many people. Everyone loves someone and/or some things.

When we love something, we want to be close to it, be involved with it, and know as much as possible about it. We use our knowledge to care for it, protect it, and look out for its welfare.

When we love someone, we strive to know their history, hopes, dreams, characteristics, abilities, likes and dislikes. We accept them as they are. We help them achieve their goals. We desire the best for them.

Such love is our prototype for understanding the practice and power of high-quality LOVE.

RELIGION

Every living person has a religion.

A person's true religion is that which gives them hope, and confidence and courage.

For some it is money, or power, or intelligence, or family, or "connections." For others it might be personality, position, cleverness, skills, status, strength, luck, personal appearance, or something else. It is what they rely on in difficult times.

In what do you place your hope?

Love works best for me.

PERFECT Love

One night, I fell asleep wondering what complete, perfect and flawless Love might be; A perfectly unflawed, right spirit; infinite understanding and wisdom; total knowledge of past, present and future; and ability to do anything, anywhere, anytime.

I awoke, terrified, in the middle of the night. My hands were shaking, I had described God! My heart was racing. I knew the name of God! God is Love! No one is supposed to know the name of God! I seriously wondered if it was time for me to leave this life, but there was no going back. I knew it was the truth.

It worked out okay. I didn't die. Everything fit together. The knowledge was equivalent to Einstein's Theory of Relativity or the long sought Unifying Theory to describe how all forms of matter and energy in the universe relate.

We are told the name of God cannot be said; there are 99 names for Allah, God is simply "I Am", the Tao that can be spoken is not the true Tao, and the Great Spirit is a great mystery. All these statements became clear when I realized God/Love is all that exists.

There is nothing that is not God/Love. Any description of God is also part of God. A true linguistic dilemma. The name of God cannot be said because it is impossible to accurately and fully do so.

FRUITS OF Love

The fruits of LOVE are inner peace,

Joy, and harmony.

MESSENGERS

It is useless to abuse the bearer of bad news.

It is equally unproductive

when appreciation for the bearer of good news

overshadows the good news itself.

FORGIVENESS (1)

Forgiveness can be a freeing, freshening, cleansing, and restorative thing for every party involved. It is an act of LOVE.

The roots of forgiveness are buried deep within the Reward and Punishment paradigm. A Reward and Punishment paradigm delivers condemnation, by self or others, of "badness". Forgiveness eliminates condemnation and opens channels of LOVE. It is a good thing, but there is an even better way when the LOVE Paradigm is in place.

LOVE does not forgive, because LOVE does not condemn. LOVE simply makes a clear-eyed assessment of the reality of the situation and of the players involved. This is followed by compassionate analysis of courses of action to improve the situation, and all involved. A desirable action will freshen, cleanse, and restore all parties. A right action frees everyone to further grow in LOVE.

LOVING assessment does not ignore the negative effects or results of a situation. Those are taken into consideration when considering an appropriate response. But the response chosen must improve everything and everyone, rather than simply punish. It must create opportunity for growth rather than simply create pain in hope of discouraging a repeat of the situation.

THINGS CHANGE

Things are what they are.

They must be acknowledged as they are,

but it is foolish to believe they must,

or will,

remain the way they are.

PRAYER

Prayer is a way of opening channels of LOVE to affect our concerns. Sometimes prayer enhances our own LOVE, sometimes other LOVE, sometimes both.

Prayers are always answered. Not always the way we expect. Not always with the result we hoped for. Always in a way that can benefit all involved if they Love well.

Be watchful for answers. LOVE well.

STRENGTH

There is the strength of a granite mountain.

The granite appears to endure unchanged by wind, heat, rain, snow, sunshine, and cold. But little by little those elements of weather reduce the stone to rocks, then sand, and finally, to dust and dirt that can nurture many kinds of life.

There is the strength of an acorn.

An acorn also endures wind, heat, rain, snow, sunshine and cold. But little by little it transforms those elements of life into a great oak tree providing shade, shelter, and food for a multitude of creatures, great and small. And after many years it, too, becomes new earth to nurture many kinds of life.

I choose the acorn?

SHOULD AND WISH

"Wish" and "Should" ride the same horse.

Should rides facing backwards

Wish rides looking forward.

The horse is made of clay.

It goes nowhere.

Love ALWAYS WINS

Everything is LOVE; although sometimes more balanced and complete than at other times. People who are strong in Knowledge, Wisdom and Action, but have major deficiencies in Right Spirit often use their talents for inappropriate purposes. We call these people Wicked or evil. We are also told of higher powers devoted to evil ways.

Such persons or powers are not to be taken lightly, but it must be recognized they stand on only three legs. They are not all-powerful. They are handicapped, although this is cleverly concealed by impressive displays of Knowledge or powerful Action. By these displays they hope to intimidate those less powerful or less knowledgeable into submitting to their control.

Balanced LOVE can see the weaknesses of an evil one and effectively counter or neutralize the effects of superior knowledge or strength. The characteristics of a strong Spirit maximize the effectiveness of available Wisdom, Knowledge and Action. The deficient Spirit of an evil one diminishes its other powers.

NOW IS ALL

Yesterday is history.
The previous hour is a memory.
The last second cannot be changed.

The next second is out of reach.
The next hour is a dream.

Only in the present moment,
can we live, learn, do, and be.

LOVE it.

IN GOD'S IMAGE

"God is LOVE, and those who live in LOVE, live in God, and God lives in them." (1 John 4:16).

Since God/LOVE includes everything that exists, that means we too are LOVE! Imperfect for sure but made of the same stuff. Made in God's image. Smaller and weaker, but part of the whole. Wired in! Permanently. No matter what!

Just like everyone else and every thing

Think about what that means. What it means to how we think about our self, about others and about the world.

THE CENTER

Life, at its center, is sweet and simple.

DO NOT BE ANXIOUS

Anxiety has two conflicting roots; (1) a belief the future cannot be controlled and (2) a belief the future must be controlled if one is to be happy.

Both beliefs, and the resulting anxiety, are incompatible with high quality LOVE.

LOVE uses all available knowledge and wisdom to act in high quality ways, with confidence that whatever the future brings, it will be an opportunity to grow in LOVE. Knowledge and wisdom certainly include considering the future effects of an action. However, LOVE recognizes and fully accepts the fact that results may be different than expected. LOVE also knows any result will provide additional learning and growth in LOVE.

Anxiety neither improves the likelihood of a desired result nor prepares one to deal with an undesired result. On the contrary, anxiety devours time and precious spiritual, intellectual and physical energy that might be applied to those purposes.

LOVE is peace.

Sin/sin

Sin, with a large "S", is a name we give to the fact physical, mental, and spiritual limitations make it impossible for humans to be perfect Love.

With a small "s", sin is the name we give to harmful actions, or inaction, resulting from Loving imperfectly.

SHOPPING SPREE

LOVE is a lot like one of those 15-minute supermarket shopping sprees people sometimes win.

We are allowed to race through a huge variety of choices, selecting some, rejecting others. Some of our selections are beneficial, others are not. Our choices are not judged; all are free, and all are ours to live with.

CHANGING BEHAVIOR

To effectively change behavior, we must focus attention on the behavior we want, then nurture and support that behavior. It works the same in personal, inter-personal, or international affairs. Hammering at a negative will not eliminate it. Only replacing it with something positive will eliminate it.

Inspired by Chick Moorman, Parent/Teacher Trainer.

PLEASURE

Happiness and pleasure are pale shadows of joy.

WHAT ABOUT BAD PEOPLE?

The attributes of LOVE include all things we admire in others and strive for in ourselves. They are what we are made of. Of course, we aren't born perfect, and even our best efforts don't ever really "get us there." We don't have enough knowledge or wisdom to always make decisions that stand the test of time. We never become strong enough or powerful enough to do all the good things we know could be done. We constantly find ourselves falling short of a completely right spirit.

These shortcomings are a result of limitations inherent in every human body, mind, and spirit. The "bad" things we do, and the "good" things we leave undone, often get us labeled.

One of those labels is "bad".

FORGIVENESS (2)

Forgiveness means learning and living in the present; not cluttering the mind and spirit with corrosive wishes, regrets or ill feelings that hinder Love. Some benefit may come to the forgiven, but the primary benefit is to the one who forgives.

It is equally important to forgive other persons, our self, and even inanimate objects.

BE AT PEACE

*"The instruction sheet began, "Assembly of Japanese bicycle require great peace of mind." *

Only a peaceful mind can maintain an unbiased view of events, develop creative options, make wise decisions, and function effectively.

In addition to that, a peaceful mind finds great joy in life.

* "Zen and the Art of Motorcycle Maintenance", Pirsig

INSUFFICIENCY

We can see farther than we can reach.

Our fundamental insufficiency is sometimes called Sin. It is the root of many problems.

Feelings of insufficiency are at the core of the human condition. They are fed by the fact our ability to perceive both needs and possibilities greatly exceeds our ability to achieve those possibilities. Even with the best of modern social sciences and technological aids, we continually fall short. Specific instances of falling short are sometimes called sins.

Our physical bodies have only limited strength and can only act in one place at a time. It is impossible for us to do everything that needs to be done.

Our knowledge of what would be good or desirable to do is constrained by the limitations of our brains, memory and emotions.

We are unable to develop sufficient wisdom to be unfailingly correct in our assessments of what is best.

Because of our body chemistry, even our spirit falls short of what we know is most desirable.

Responses to personal insufficiency are many. Some drive themselves compulsively for perfection. Some create a personal illusion of personal perfection. Some become cynical about their fellow humans.

Some are overwhelmed by guilt. Some sink into frustration and despair. Some hate themselves. Some seek comfort in exposing the shortcomings of others.

It's a bleak picture when we focus on insufficiencies.

However, the beauty of all this is that, even though we are born almost completely insufficient, we learn, and we grow in right spirit, knowledge, wisdom and ability to act. We grow in Love; we become higher and higher levels of Love.

As we grow in Love, we grow in our understanding of what Perfect Love might be. And as we come to understand that, we also come to understand our "insufficiencies" do not represent dreadful failure but rather, serve to illuminate what we can become, what might be.

We come to understand Perfect Love does not demand total sufficiency, or perfection; does not demand anything. We realize Perfect Love generously offers opportunities for us to learn and to grow, in strength, knowledge, spirit and wisdom. Perfect Love created us, accepts us, desires only the best for us and celebrates our growth in Love.

CHANGE

For most mortals, change has five steps;

1. "Ohhh, No!"

2. "Stupid, idiot, ___(whatever)___!"

3. "Ahhh-ha!"

4. "Oh, Wow!"

5. "Hey, what if ....?"

      ......then someone else says, "Ohh, No!"

A friend observed that, in their workplace, change does not always reach the "Ahhh-ha!" stage.

SEE THINGS AS THEY ARE

"If you stop seeing the world in terms of what you like

and what you dislike.

and see things for what they truly are

in themselves,

you will find a great deal more peace in your life."

Patrick Jane, "The Mentalist," CBS, Nov. 12, 2009

GARDENS

On a beautiful spring day, two gardeners prepared the soil in hopes of bountiful fall harvests.

The first gardener flung extravagant quantities of mixed seeds on the loose soil and pressed them into place. The second gardener carefully spaced individual seeds in straight, labeled rows.

As green sprouts first broke through the warm ground both gardeners began tending their plots.

The first gardener carefully tended the healthiest sprouts wherever they grew, loosening the soil around them, making sure they had room to grow, with plenty of sunshine and water. In some places scrawny weeds took root, unnoticed amidst the profusion of flourishing flowers and vegetables. Harvesting the garden became a search through the many types of plants to find desired vegetables or flowers, but the effort was always richly rewarded.

Through the spring and summer, the second gardener diligently searched out weeds among the growing plants and destroyed every one in sight. At harvest time the garden was triumphantly tidy and weed free. The ground was packed hard from frequent searches and many desirable plants had been damaged or destroyed as nearby weeds were removed; but each surviving flower and vegetable was a sweet reminder of the gardener's triumph over the weeds.

We are all gardeners.

BE Love? OR DO Love?

BE

(Think about it.)

HELPLESSNESS

We are empowered by LOVE. We need never feel helpless. By LOVING well, we are empowered to extract value from any situation, often by modifying the situation, sometimes by understanding it, and sometimes by learning or growing in other ways.

OPTIMISM (1)

I believe in possibilities. I understand the world as an imperfect place, but I also have confidence Love grows, and there is positive potential in every situation.

Considering that unrealistic and overly optimistic, people sometimes tell me to lower my expectations, so I won't be disappointed.

So, I ask, "When was the last time you were really upset? When your car wouldn't start? When your child did not follow the rules? When your plane was late?" Nearly all laugh and have a ready answer.

Then I say, "Why were you upset? What caused you to believe your car would start every time, your child would unfailingly follow the rules, or your plane would always be on time?"

And then, "Which of us is unrealistic and overly optimistic?"

Love NEVER CHANGES

Love knows of change,

but because Love exists only in the present moment,

Love never experiences change.

DEALING WITH DIFFICULT PEOPLE

It is impossible for any person to LOVE perfectly. Limitations of our physical minds and bodies prevent us from knowing everything, or doing everything, or always being right.

We cannot know every bit of knowledge in the world, to say nothing of knowledge not yet discovered. We can only be in one place at a time and cannot survive in some places.

We can, at best, only act effectively on a relatively small scale in one place at one time. In addition, our body chemistry and imperfect wisdom prevent us from having a completely right spirit.

To deal effectively with another person, whether friend or "foe", one must thoroughly discern, understand, and accept the reality of their strengths and weaknesses.

We must LOVE them.

DUTY (3)

"Duty" is a wolf in sheep's clothing.

Dressed in good causes,

but powered by debt and guilt

instead of LOVE.

It feeds on good intentions.

FREEDOM

Be your best you, regardless of what anyone or anything does to you, or for you. Live life 100%. Love it all. Enjoy!

It seems to me, that is true freedom.

BE WHERE YOU ARE

Be entirely where you are. Anything else is futile.

Wishing you were someplace else or doing something else is a tremendous waste of time and energy; it diverts precious resources of mind and spirit from the present situation, which is the only situation you can affect anyway.

LOVE where you are. Accept it, know it, learn it, and understand it. Act on it wisely. It will serve you well.

MAGIC BOTTLES

Two children, upon coming of age, were each given a magic bottle exactly half filled with clear, sweet ambrosia. Both children tasted the ambrosia and, delighting in its rich flavor, set out to fill their bottles to the top. However, no matter how much ambrosia was put into a magic bottle, the level did not change.

Bitterly complaining that the bottle remained half-empty, the first child resolved to preserve the remaining precious liquid in a safe place. The strategy was successful. However, as time passed the hidden ambrosia became dark and cloudy and bitter.

The second child, resolving to enjoy her gift, drank deeply of the ambrosia and shared it generously with friends, only to discover the bottle magically remained half filled with an increasingly delightful liquid.

Life is like that.

LIFE IS LOVE

Life is LOVE.

Live 100%.

LOVE it all.

HARMONY

LOVE is like surfing, skiing, getting on an escalator, or being part of a musical group. All require knowledge of the "rules of the game" and the skill to blend into them. All are pleasant when done well, otherwise, who knows?

Quality LOVE results in harmony, internal and external. Things work out well. This is not because rewards are dispensed by a remote authority, but because we are utilizing the power that frames the entire system and fitting smoothly into that system.

Low quality LOVE results in disharmony, discord and discomfort, not because punishment is imposed by a watchful authority, but simply because things just don't work out well when we resist or ignore reality.

LOVE is the reality.

THE NAME OF GOD

The whole world is part of the name of God.

The universe is part of the name of God.

The smallest flower or tadpole is

part of the name of God.

A complex chemical reaction

is part of the name of God.

A city is part of the name of God.

A song is part of the name of God.

My neighbor is part of the name of God.

Even I, am part of the name of God.

WHO WILL SAY

The role of Religion is to advocate personal beliefs for individual and common good.

The role of Government is to regulate, for the common good, interactions between individuals, between individuals and the government, and between governments.

Trouble begins when either crosses over.

THE GREATEST COMMANDMENTS

Love God (Love) with all your heart,

and all your soul,

and all your mind.

The second is this;

Love your neighbor and yourself,

equally.

A paraphrase of Matthew 22:37-39

WISDOM

Wisdom is the ability to make choices that, over time, prove to be positive, effective and helpful for all concerned.

One who possesses wisdom generally has above average knowledge, understanding, experience, and an intuitive understanding in many areas, particularly human behavior. That person has a mind that is open to, and seeks out, many ways of looking at a situation. Combined with these traits is an ability to "run the movie forward" exploring various future ramifications of a statement or action. Finally, that person must have a very generous, caring, spirit to be truly Wise.

GOALS

A worthy goal

requires no compromise

in the quality of our LOVE.

EDUCATING AND GROWING

It is usually not difficult to identify, in our self or in others, opportunities for growth in Knowledge, Wisdom, Spirit, or Action. It is always more difficult to become aware of strengths in those areas because we are conditioned to look for imperfections. But strengths are always present and are seeds for improvement. A quality LOVE approach to the person and the issues will make clear how best to use available resources.

DUALITY

The concept of duality breeds much mischief. LOVE and evil are no more separate than heat and cold, or light and dark.

Varying degrees of heat are called hot, warm, cool, cold, frigid, etc.

Varying degrees of light are called bright, dim, shadow, shade, darkness, etc.

In the same way, there is only LOVE in varying degrees of quality, which we call caring, generous, saintly, big-hearted, loving, kindly, ignorant, careless, lazy, stupid, naughty, mean, wicked, perverted, evil, etc.

Weakness or strength in Spirit, or Action, or Knowledge, or Wisdom; each has its own name and may be considered "good", or "bad" or "it depends"

TAKE CARE

Beware what you set your heart upon,

for it could well become yours.

Modern ancient proverb

THE WATERS

"Come to me, come home to the sea," a deep voice rumbled upward through the mist on the mountainside.

"Let's go, let's go to the sea," bubbled the mountain stream.

The tranquil meadow pond replied, "I cannot come with you now. I will be along in good time, but now it is time for me to be still."

Leaping and splashing the stream cried out, "Hurry and join me. It is our duty to return to the sea. It is our destiny. Don't you agree?"

"Yes, I agree," reflected the pond, "A journey to the sea is our destiny and our ever-present tendency, but I have no duty, only opportunities, to move towards my destiny, towards the sea."

The pond continued quietly, "My opportunities must be received and dealt with in whatever way best serves myself and the world. We each grow and contribute in our own way. I must decide for myself what way that is."

"But it is good, it is our duty," frothed the stream, scurrying through tree roots near the shore.

"Go in joy and peace," murmured the pond, "Do your part. For now, for me, this is the place to be."

DREAMS

With so much material world around us it is easy to forget everything that is, was first a dream; an idea that came unbidden from who knows where.

Respect dreams, they often speak of things we cannot reach by the stepping stones of logic and experience.

PATIENT Love

Perfect LOVE knows the limitations of individuals, and desires only the best for them. From this desire, "rules" arise as guidance toward harmonious, happy, productive lives.

These "rules" are caring advice, not lines drawn in the sand for retribution.

Negative results that arise from ignoring the "rules" are natural consequences of imperfect (low quality) LOVE. They are not punishment imposed from above.

THINGS ARE WHAT THEY ARE

Too often we are unable to deal effectively with a situation because we are angry or disappointed with it. We tend to focus on what we wish it is, or isn't, instead of seeing what it actually is.

We must be rigorously honest and thorough in looking at any situation if we are to deal with it effectively.

WHAT TO DO?

Decisions, decisions! How to decide what to do? What will be best? So many choices! It's enough to make me crazy.

It seems there's never enough information to be sure a decision will be "right", or "best". Yet, decisions must be made and are sometimes made by default. Doing nothing is a decision.

The real issue here is *not*, "I want to know what to do." The *real* issue is, "I need to be confident." (in my decisions)

Solid confidence arises only from the decision-making process, not from outcomes. Outcomes are unreliable sources of confidence. They are often not "good", and "good" outcomes often come as much from luck as from skill, talent or wisdom.

So, what is a good process? A good process needs as much knowledge as possible, and fair, kind and honest consideration of all facts, including potential outcomes. It needs wisdom to evaluate the potential results of various choices and to choose the most desirable one. It needs the courage and ability to carry out the chosen decision.

Hm-m-m, knowledge, a right spirit, wisdom and action. That is LOVE!

The most effective process is to LOVE the situation as well as possible. Only then can we be confident we have done all we can do – and are prepared to deal effectively with any unexpected results.

One more thing we have going for us. Although our Love is limited and imperfect, we are connected to the support and care of Perfect Love (God) that will help us make "good" of whatever comes. We call that germ of Perfect Love within each of us our "conscience", "gut feeling", "spirit", or "heart". Whatever we call it, it is in every person, waiting to be recognized and utilized.

Love is all we do. Love is all we are. Not complete or perfect, but able to learn and grow. Our opportunity and challenge is to learn and grow Love by doing and being Love to the best of our ability.

It can be scary at times, or frustrating, but it grows confidence and it grows joy within and without.

As frequently stated in the Bible, "Do not be afraid." I shall go in peace and confidence.

I am Love.

FORGIVENESS (3)

Forgiveness is an essential lifestyle.

Forgiveness is Love, pure and simple.
It is an utter absence of desire for payback.

Forgiveness desires "better" for all concerned.

By living forgiveness, we learn
what forgiveness looks like and feels like.

We begin to understand
God's infinite and relentless Love (forgiveness).

We enjoy peace and strength
in this harmony with God.

Forgiveness is not ignoring or forgetting what has happened but acknowledging it and moving on in a way to bring all concerned closer to God.

INCOMPREHENSIBLE Love

In this world, our intellectual and perceptual capacities are so limited we cannot fully comprehend perfect LOVE.

It is quite reasonable to believe there are dimensions to LOVE we cannot perceive or even imagine.

That might be just as well, since we have our hands full utilizing what little we do know.

TRUTH (3)

We know no whole truths, only partial truths.

Trouble begins when partial truths

are mistaken for whole ones.

GIVING AND RECEIVING

It is important for people to be kind and thoughtful and generous to others. It is important to the individual and to the world. It is equally important people are gracious, joyful and appreciative recipients of all that comes to them. This, too, is important to the individual and to the world.

It is a matter of balance – a matter of sharing joy. Without the constant flow of both giving and receiving the entire system clogs up and goes bad. The world becomes dark and sour.

Where there are generous givers, receivers and the world use and multiply the skills, talents, knowledge and gifts of the generous person. Bonds of mutual support strengthen the world. And the skills, talents, knowledge and gifts of those generous persons multiply as they are used and appreciated by others.

Where there are gracious receivers, generosity has an outlet and givers' horizons are expanded to the greater opportunities and glories of the world. Receivers gain helpful skills, talents and knowledge and become engaged in the opportunities and glories of the world. Joy is gained on both sides.

Being a gracious, joyful and appreciative receiver is another form of giving. It gives pleasure, joy and encouragement to the giver.

FAITH

Faith

is simply a deep seated, unshakable, confidence

in the power, presence, "rightness", and effectiveness

of LOVE

in every situation.

FREEDOM

The sweetest, most desired freedom,

freedom from fear,

is the least often obtained,

yet the most accessible.

POSSIBILITIES

Unlike "lower" animals, we humans are aware our abilities and actions are less than perfect and can be improved.

Our ability to perceive possibilities exceeds our ability to achieve those possibilities.

Guilt can be one result, progress can be another.

Choose well.

JOY

The fruit of LOVE is joy so achingly huge it overflows human capacity, obliterating mere pleasure, pain, and happiness.

Its companion is deep sorrow for those not yet knowing that joy.

ACCEPT, BELIEVE, UNDERSTAND

Understanding, belief and acceptance are
very different things.

The presence of one in no way assures either of the
others will be present or will follow.

Acceptance is a matter of the Spirit.

Belief is a matter of Knowledge.

Understanding is a matter of Wisdom.

Ideally, but rarely, all three are present
and operate in concert.

THAT'S LIFE

Change is another word for life.

ALL THINGS WORK FOR GOOD

All things work for good in those who LOVE well.

In every situation,

high quality LOVE finds opportunities

to learn, grow, advance toward its goals,

and grow LOVE in the world.

FEELINGS

Feelings are real, miserable, delightful,

valid, free, and wild,

sources of information.

They must be recognized and respected,

but must not, alone, dictate action.

LIES

A popular and very successful High School math teacher, when asked how he turned out so many high performing math students, replied in a conspiratorial tone, "I lie to them." Then explained with a smile, "I tell them they are really good at it, and soon they are."

Did he lie? Or did he simply allow for possibilities as yet unseen? Did he lie? Or did he simply mobilize abilities even the student was not aware of?

Chick Moorman teaches parents and teachers that talking about unwanted behavior is counter-productive because the child leaves the conversation with a head full of the prohibited behavior. Instead, he recommends clearly stating only the desired behavior, so the child visualizes behaving in that way.

Hmm-m-m, could the most effective way be to allow for, and encourage, the best possible outcome – even when it's hard to imagine it ever happening?

Would that work for adult interactions? Could blunt or angry criticism be deflected or neutralized by responding as though it arose from kind intentions? Or maybe it did. What would it cost to operate under that assumption? What would be lost? What might be gained? Would that be a lie?

Would it be a lie to be gracious to an unpleasant person when you would rather give them a piece of your mind? What would be lost? What might be gained?

Of course, there are times painful facts must be brought forward but they are most effective when delivered with compassion and support. Quality Love leaves space for unseen possibilities and tells the truth in ways that grow all involved in positive ways.

IN SYNCH

"There was more to Bilbo Baggins than even he knew."
Lord of the Rings, J.R.R. Tolkien

It is just the same with each of us. The LOVE of which we are made, the LOVE at our core, provides wisdom, strength and courage to be more than we imagine.

When we are in tune with the Love within us, the Love within others, and with infinite Love, we find pain and frustration being displaced by peace and joy and great effectiveness.

It's almost like magic.

WHY DO BAD THINGS HAPPEN TO GOOD PEOPLE?

Two things are wrong with this question:

1. There is no reason "bad things" should <u>not</u> happen to "good" people. "Good" does not mean perfect.

People who generally LOVE well are known as "good", and it is true higher quality LOVE yields higher levels of harmony, peace and productivity. The catch is; no one can LOVE perfectly and achieve perfect results, perfect harmony and perfect peace.

Limitations of our physical body and mind make it certain no one has enough knowledge and wisdom to be unfailingly correct in determining the short-range and long-range effects of their decisions. No one has enough knowledge and physical ability to perfectly perform everything it would be good to do.

No one can make entirely appropriate decisions every time, and nobody's motives are totally pure. We are all imperfect, so we all get imperfect and unexpected results. Sometimes they are better than expected (good) and sometimes they are worse (bad).

2. "Bad things" usually means things that cause discomfort or fail to satisfy our desires or expectations. Is there any reason we should expect uninterrupted comfort? And, given the limited knowledge and wisdom that create our desires and expectations, why should we believe satisfying them would produce results we would be happy with?

NOTE: *It is important to remember all things work towards "good" in those who LOVE well. Everything may not meet our expectations or wishes but there are always opportunities for learning, growth and service in every situation.*

NOT QUITE

Total disaster never quite arrives.

Because
LOVE always finds a way to keep on.

UNHAPPINESS

The only cause of unhappiness is
unrealistic expectations.

For what reason should we expect any person or thing to
be perfect, or to unfailingly meet our hopes or
expectations?

COURTESY and COMPASSION

Courtesy and compassion lubricate the gears of society.
The closer the gears, and the greater the pressure,
the greater the need for this lubrication.
Without it the gears squeal, screech and
grind each other to powder.

Courtesy is helping, and requesting, rather than
demanding, regardless of others' "duty."

Compassion is recognizing the need for help,
seeing through others' eyes, realizing that seemingly
inappropriate actions are sometimes
reasonable responses to
issues, information,
or events we are not aware of.

TRUE OR FALSE?

False love between two people
is a relationship
based on a consuming desire
to possess and control the other.

Like two mirrors facing each other,
coming closer and closer
to exclude all but each other,
finally closing against each other
with only darkness between.

True love is like two mirrors facing each other
with a candle between.

It's warmth and light reflecting back and forth,
growing and growing,
until it overflows into the world.

The candle is LOVE.

ONLY Love WORKS WELL

Only LOVE works.

Study LOVE.

Pursue LOVE.

Trust LOVE.

Be excellent LOVE.

EDUCATION

Reward and punishment

are the lowest forms of education.

Chuang-tzu
369 B.C -286 B.C.

COMFORT

When life is hard, or we are grieving,
it is good to know Perfect LOVE (God)
knows how we are feeling.

Because Perfect Love already knows
how we are made, and treasures us,
we can pour out our hearts
without fear of dismissal or condemnation.

We can be confident
Perfect LOVE is accessible to us
and will break through the darkness
with the comfort and growth of LOVE.

Be watchful.
Look and listen.
LOVE comes
in unexpected ways.

HATRED

Like Evil,
Hatred arises
from a grossly deformed Spirit
and can be quite powerful.

Unlike Evil,
Hatred suffers serious deficiencies
of both knowledge and wisdom.

Hatred
closes the mind
and thrives in the darkness
of ignorance.

As a result,
Hatred is not able
to effectively understand
those it opposes,
or those it seeks as allies.

In the end,
Hatred is overcome
by higher quality Love.

RELIGION OR PHILOSOPHY?

A philosophy is a group of thoughts and ideas organized by a set of logical rules that provide internal consistency and organization.

A religion is a group of thoughts, ideas, and beliefs relied upon by an individual for strength, hope, and wisdom in every aspect of their life. It is the foundation upon which a life is constructed.

The difference is primarily a matter of belief and lies only within an individual.

Christianity, Judaism, Islam and Buddhism are religions to some and philosophies to others. Marxism, existentialism and capitalism are philosophies to some and religions to others.

There are those who claim a leap (or leaps) of (blind) faith is the difference between religion and philosophy. This claim provides a convenient, smoke-shrouded dumping ground for questions or concerns about those tenets or practices of a "religion" that might be irregular, inconsistent or immoral. The claim is the best refuge of the charlatan and the poorly grounded.

NOTE: This does not mean leaps of faith/belief cannot be real or productive. Often, a leap of faith opens the way to greater understanding and growth. A God of Love has made us capable of both leaps of faith, and logical thought processes. Both are intended to be used, not alone, but together with a right spirit, knowledge, wisdom, and appropriate action.

OPTIMISM (2)

Optimism is often (mis)understood to be a denial of reality, a view of the world that ignores harsh facts of life in this world.

In truth, optimism recognizes and accepts the facts of imperfection in the world and its inhabitants. Optimism does deny the premise that events and persons will inevitably continue as in the past; a premise often put forward by pessimists presenting themselves as realists.

When one is convinced present patterns and actions will, or must, inevitably continue; exploration and development are discouraged or viewed as useless.

Facts of the past are undeniable and must be recognized, explored and mined for information to enhance the positive and minimize the unproductive as we go forward into an uncertain future, that we can affect.

Love VS. REWARD & PUNISHMENT

A Reward & Punishment paradigm
generates fear, greed, selfishness, self-centeredness,
narrow-mindedness, defensiveness

A LOVE paradigm
generates compassion, open-mindedness, courage,
generosity, creativity, self-improvement, and . . . . .

FLOGGING WEEDS

Flowers are not created by flogging weeds.

FOR OR AGAINST

It is almost always easier to be against something than to be for something better.

"Against" is easy to do and easy to "sell".
- "Against" sees only problems.
- "Against" has a clearly defined target.
- "Against" imagines terrible outcomes.
- "Against" creates strange bedfellows, with little in common outside their current antagonism.
- "Against" tears down.
- When successful, "Against" creates a void, which often fills with worse mischief.
- "Against" fosters hatred – its ultimate form.
- "Against" has little hope of changing its opponents because it is unable to clearly see who they are, and why they are the way they are.

"For" is difficult to do and difficult to "sell"
- "For" sees possibilities that must be imagined.
- "For" must find or create specific supportive allies.
- "For" envisions opportunities.
- "For" builds up.
- When successful, "For" creates or maintains something others can build upon.
- At its best, "For" grows individuals and connects people for mutual good.

Strive always to be "For".

HOPE

Hope is not simply wishful thinking.

Hope is abiding confidence

LOVE has potential

to make the future

better than the present.

TRANSITIONS

We leave the security of the womb unhappy and fearful at entering a strange, uncomfortable world, only to discover it filled with unimagined delights.

Isn't it interesting that, when our journey here is complete, we often depart as unhappy and fearful of the next strange, uncomfortable world as we were of this one.

Could we be wrong again?

NOTES FOR CHRISTIANS

THE GREATEST COMMANDMENTS

LOVE God (LOVE) with all your heart, and all your soul,
and all your mind.

The second is this; LOVE your neighbor and yourself,
equally.
A paraphrase of Matthew 22:37-39

I give you a new commandment: LOVE one another.
As I have LOVED you, so you must LOVE one another.
John 13:34

Love is universal and underlies all religions. I grew up
in a Christian community, so I have some specific thoughts
to share with Christians and those studying Christianity.

Suzanne

Notes

DEAR READER (2)

Folks come to God from many places and by many routes. This is not surprising since God is in everything and in everybody (because everything and everybody has come from God)

Hints of God are always present, ready to be observed. As we observe, we each become aware of God in unique ways that work for us.

Before I backed into God, I had come to know much *about* God through years of Sunday school, and church attendance, but I did not *know* God very well. I did not understand how God fit into everything, including me. I was puzzled about where prayers went and why God mattered. I had learned much about what different people think about God, how they see God at work, and how they worship God, but I still puzzled over who God *is*.

I was not thinking about that big question at all when, with Hugh, I unwittingly took the first step on a long road.

I share this section, not because I believe my path will work for you – it will not, but in the hope something from my path might illuminate yours.

We are each on our own – but never alone.

Keep smiling, Love it all.

A DILEMMA

Much of contemporary Christianity rides the horns of a dilemma. The horns are: Belief in an all-powerful, compassionate, merciful, and unconditionally loving God willing to sacrifice God's only Son for our salvation. And at the same time, believing that without that salvation we will be eternally rejected by that same God, and beyond the reach of God's presence.

The root of this dilemma lies not in the nature of God, but in misunderstanding the nature of God's LOVE. This misunderstanding weakens our faith, our theology, and our will.

We say God's grace is free and universally available, yet we consistently use terms of reward and punishment, debt and payment, which imply God's LOVE is NOT infinite or unconditional. Terms such as atonement, redemption and penitence often suggest punishment and reward, debt and payment.

It cannot be both ways – God's acceptance and LOVE for us either depends on certain conditions or it is absolutely free.

Frequently, this conflict is dealt with by disregarding one possibility or the other, by citing the unfathomable nature of God, or by simply ignoring the entire issue.

There is a better way. Read on.

GOD

We all talk about God and we all have an idea what or who God is; and each person's idea is different, and subject to change. That is to be expected since people are complex, and God is too big for anyone to completely comprehend.

However, even though no one can completely comprehend the details of God, we can comprehend the framework and essence of God.

A most helpful and productive way to understand and know God is as Perfect LOVE.

PERFECT Love

What if there was Infinite Knowledge of everything past, present, and future? Infinite ability to Act (create, modify, or destroy) simultaneously in all times and places? What if there was Infinite Wisdom to always use that power and knowledge exactly the right way for perfectly right purposes? And a Perfectly Right Spirit combining patience, understanding and compassion with the infinite Wisdom, Knowledge, and Action?

This is a description of God! This is what it really means when we say God is Love, rather than the more common, but limited, understanding that God is "kindly and loving"

God is perfect, infinite Love and we are imperfect, limited versions of that same Love. We, too, are Spirit, Knowledge, Wisdom and Action. We are made in God's image. A shadowy, imperfect image, but made of the same stuff. And, we have the capacity to grow more like the perfect and infinite image. As we gain new knowledge, mature in spirit, gain wisdom through experience, and acquire greater physical capabilities, we become higher quality Love.

It is a grand mystery that Love (God), which is already infinite, can increase, but that is what happens as the Love that is us grows.

NAMING GOD

There is danger here. Having learned words about *God, we must not believe we now know all there is to know about God. We do not, and can never, know the full dimensions of God. God is more than we can fully comprehend or imagine. A mystery remains. We can always learn more, but we will never, in this life, know more than the shadows.*

WHERE IS GOD?

God has a place in most everyone's mind even though many may not have thought about it. For some, "God is in His heaven", for others, "God is always beside me", or "God is 'there' for me". Even for those who say, "There is no God" (as they imagine God might be). The variations are endless, and they have profound effects on our lives.

A common element is that God is "somewhere else". Possibly far away, possibly in the bleachers cheering us on, possibly close by offering advice, maybe even lending a helping hand. Many possible locations but always external to us; Caring, but separate. It is not so.

Perfect Love (God) is nothing less than infinite action, perfect wisdom, infinite knowledge, and perfectly right spirit. Everything that exists is necessarily a sub-set of those perfect and infinite characteristics – incomplete and imperfect but made of the same stuff. We are each part of God and God is part of us. We are imperfect and incomplete, but we are Love and we are directly connected to Perfect Love (God).

We do not need to call for God to come and help, God is here, we only need to learn to see and hear and do what Love teaches. We can also learn from the germ of Love in others if we make the effort to recognize it and strengthen it. And, of course, all of creation has much to teach us about the Perfect Love it is made of.

Again, God is not separate from people. God did not make us kind of like God, then go away.

The perception that God is someplace separate from people leads to all manner of trouble, including the subversive idea our shortcomings must be "punished" or "paid for" in order to "reunite" us with God. The presence of God cannot be bought. It is not a reward. It is a fact. Every one of us is not just precious *to* God, we are precious *parts* of God. God will not leave us. God cannot leave us.

When we eliminate the perception of separation, we can better know and benefit from all dimensions of God's Love. We have direct access to strength, spirit, knowledge and wisdom beyond imagination. We are made of it; we can tap directly into it.

Knowing we are (imperfect) parts of God can give us courage and confidence to see life as opportunities to expand and grow in ways that are beneficial to others and to ourselves. There is great peace, harmony, strength and joy in being aware of, and tapping into, the infinite capabilities of God even though we cannot fully comprehend them.

Caution: Using the powers of LOVE (Spirit, Knowledge, Wisdom, Action) for anything except growing LOVE creates highly destructive disharmony within and without.

OUT OF THE BOX

Understanding God as the source of rewards and punishments puts God in a box. It confines God to the status of rule maker and score-keeper. It also puts us into a box, playing an anxious game with one eye, and much of our mind, on the scoreboard.

Knowing God as Love frees God from the box, revealing God as the infinite source of inspiration, creativity, wisdom and strength. The infinite source of all good.

Knowing God as Love also frees us from a box. Outside the box we can devote all our attention and effort to living fully. Free from fear. Free from striving to master a game we are doomed to lose. Free to tap the Love within. Free to become more than we ever imagined. Free to do seemingly impossible things and to know peace and joy beyond our wildest dreams.

GOD DEMANDS NOTHING.

God demands nothing.

God offers (gives) everything,

God rejoices over good choices.

THE NATURE OF GOD – Q & A

Q: Does forgiveness mean God excuses sin?
A: No.   God does not cease to be God.
Although God is merciful to the sinner, God does not
excuse the evil of sin, for to forgive is not to excuse.

The Study Catechism/Confirmation Version
(Presbyterian Church USA).

Q: It's that last sentence – I can't stop thinking all this "Love "" stuff is lulling us into a false sense of security.

A: There is not much security in believing God is going to "get you".   Real security is knowing that, although God is fully aware of the harmful effects of every sin, God is still on our side helping us become the best we can be.

Q: Then I get confused about Jesus dying for our sins. The Original Sin, or our sins committed here on earth?

A: Yes.   Both.   Jesus died so we could get over being afraid of God and get close enough to understand God and let God help us.   We have the perfect partner.   Love understands Original Sin as our inability to measure up to the perfection of God; unable because we are finite and physical, and it is impossible for us to possess, or even be totally aware of. the dimensions and perfection of God. God made us this way for reasons of God's own and Loves us as God's own.

Q: What about "to forgive is not to excuse?"

A: Actions have consequences. To forgive is to forego vengeance; it does not erase damage done or the fact of damage done.

There is great joy and freedom in knowing the nature of God is entirely positive. God creates and nurtures. We are made in His image although we are a dim and incomplete image and subject to all kinds of unintentional and intentional errors of thought, word and deed, causing all manner of trouble for us and the world.

Whatever we do, God just wants us to know God, come to God, learn from God and grow more like God so we can be better, happier people growing LOVE in the world.

JESUS' PLACE

The most persistent and insidious misbelief of human beings is the belief in right and wrong. (The "knowledge" of, or belief in, Good and Evil.)

Accompanying this belief in right and wrong is the equally strong belief wrong/evil will be/is/must be, punished and right/good will be rewarded. (Probably based upon observations that results of wrong/evil are frequently undesirable and right/good frequently provides helpful results.)

These two beliefs are virtually unquestioned in most cultures and, in fact, have provided a precarious sort of order in this world. Unfortunately, these beliefs have also led to punitive means of socialization and, worst of all, the misbelief that an all-knowing, all-powerful God is an all-knowing, all-powerful punisher – and rewarder. Within such a paradigm, the concept of pure LOVE becomes almost incomprehensible.

Although God's relentless LOVE is all-encompassing, we "just don't get it". So, an all-powerful God who knows there has been no crime, and no heavenly requirement, has said, "Okay, if you need a sacrifice before you will/can believe yourselves acceptable to Me, I'll do it for all of you and get it over with."

So, God, who is no less than perfect LOVE and will not/cannot reject any of His creation, comes to God's creation as a perfect person to demonstrate perfect LOVE and suffer the ultimate human punishment to satisfy, not God's judgment, but people's mistaken judgment that they are unacceptable to God.

If there were headlines, they would read:
"COMPLETELY FAULTLESS MAN PAYS ULTIMATE
PENALTY TO GAIN FREEDOM FOR
SELF-IMPRISONED PEOPLE."

It is right to be full of joy and thanks for such generous LOVE. It is also natural to strive to know, and to better be, that same LOVE and to generously share it.

CONDITIONING

Three lessons for Christians.

1) Conditioning and practice are important.

2) No prize is awarded for the amount of conditioning and practice.

3) Performance is the prize.

Biblical teachings are the conditioning prescription for Christians. Over and over Jesus reminds us our prize comes, not from how well we follow "rules", but from what we become as a result of practicing what the "rules" teach us. Like a musician or athlete, our practice sessions are often imperfect, but over time repetition builds both endurance and skill. With practice, better performance becomes second nature and we are free to reach even higher.

Practice, practice, practice, but rather than becoming proud of your practice, be joyful in your growth as a child of God.

WORSHIP & PRAISE

We all understand it does no good to abuse a messenger who brings bad news. What is more difficult to grasp is; it is not helpful to *appreciate* a bearer of *good* news so greatly the news is not fully utilized. This happens in all walks of life but is a particular hazard for Christians

We owe Christ overwhelming awe, respect and appreciation for bringing the best news of all (and for paying the highest price for being the messenger) but we disrespect His efforts if we do not give great attention to the message of Love that He lived and taught.

Christ did not seek praise or glory. He sought hearts and lives for the Love that is God. He sought to lead hearts and lives to learn Love, do Love and most of all, to be Love.

Give praise and be the Love that is God.

He came singing LOVE.
  He lived singing LOVE.
    He died singing LOVE.
      If the song is to continue,
        we must do the singing.
(seen on a church banner)

CHRIST

To help people know God is always entirely accessible to them, Christ taught and demonstrated LOVE. He suffered punishment people believe they deserve, so people can know it is safe to be with God.

This omniscient, omnipotent, omnipresent God of Love recognizes and understands ("forgives", in the punishment tradition) people's shortcomings and seeks to increase their understanding and practice of LOVE, in order to bring them closer to God (Perfect LOVE).

It is God's nature to want only the best for us, and to be terribly wounded by the awful things we inflict upon ourselves and others, sometimes even when doing our best to do "good". Then, feeling guilty for being inadequate or "bad", we feel we deserve punishment to "pay" or "atone" for our "shortcomings."

Likewise, we come to desire punishment of others who have been "bad". We even mobilize, personally or collectively, to fight "bad", squandering much energy and attention.

Wallowing around in "bad" stuff is an old, old trap and it doesn't illuminate much or improve much of anything. LOVE is a much more productive way to view and live life.

For all of time, God has tried in myriad ways to teach God's LOVE and God's acceptance, but our human "good and evil/reward and punishment" filter perceives guidance as, "Do it or die – if not immediately, then later!"

It is humbling to think Christ suffered and died as payment to God for the all the Sin and sins of all people. But that was not the reason. The real reason is even more incredible.

Christ did indeed die to save us, not from the wrath of God, but from ourselves. Christ's death was not a cosmic "deal" to change God's mind, to purchase God's acceptance of us. Nothing is necessary for that. God does not demand payment. God only wants us in God's arms – for our own good. The chilling fact is Christ's death was necessary only to change *our* minds and hearts.

Now we are free to most effectively live LOVE, and grow LOVE, in our self and in the world.

GRACE

(a letter to a friend)

Grace is a strange business. When we are down here looking upward, it doesn't make sense. It doesn't fit our experience. It has been helpful for me to try to get a glimpse of it from another side.

A dog adopted us many years ago. We referred to him as "Fierce Clifford the Wonder Dog" although the only danger was – you might be licked to death.

Clifford had a mind of his own. We believe he lived independently for some time before adopting us. We worked hard to teach him how to make his way safely in the world. He patiently endured our efforts, and sometimes accommodated them.

Clifford never did catch- on to walking on a leash. He would constantly strain excitedly at the leash, choking and coughing while tugging us along. Upon arrival at our destination he always looked so pleased with himself, as though his efforts alone had brought us there.

Clifford never learned to stay safely in the yard, so he had to be on a tether when outside. However, he and the cat learned if he pushed the screen door with his nose while the cat jumped on his back and pulled the latch lever down, both could be free for a while.

And so, it came to pass Clifford and an automobile had a disagreement over who would have the right-of-way. Clifford lost, at the cost of a shattered thigh bone.

A veterinary surgeon placed all the pieces in their proper positions and immobilized the leg with a cast, which Clifford chewed to pieces.

Another cast was attached and painted with Tabasco sauce, but Clifford just drank a lot of water while chewing the cast to pieces. Yet another cast, and a fancy pie plate collar, finally got him through to full recovery and he lived many more healthy and unrepentant years.

Writing this I realize it illustrates several parallels to our relationship with God – except being tethered or on a leash. Those are subjects for another day. My point today is our family's reaction to Clifford's foolish, reckless folly. We did not scold or punish him, we did what most anyone would do; we comforted him and did everything we could to help him recover. I think that's Grace – just caring. That's what God does – always. I think it is easier to feel than it is to understand logically.

When we try to understand Grace logically our life experiences of "action equals reaction," "actions have consequences," and "reward and punishment," make it very difficult to comprehend unqualified, unconditional Love – even though we often spontaneously live it as we respond to emergencies, tragedies or disasters.

HEAVEN AND HELL

Paradise is real. Outer darkness with weeping and gnashing of teeth is also real, but people don't get sent there, they go there.

God wants us home.

After death, without the restraints of physical mind and body, each of us will be fully aware of perfect, infinite Love. Enfolded by that Love, we will clearly see, cascading through time, the positive and negative effects of all our actions and inactions.

Joy will come as we see unexpected positive results. There will also be the sorrow of knowing every harmful effect of our human limitations. The sorrow will only be relieved by opening ourselves to the perfect peace of God's unconditional welcome, consolation and LOVE. God's open arms always await us.

On the other hand, if we are convinced all-knowing God could not accept our unworthy, undeserving self and walk or run away in pride, shame or fear, we shall exist in unrelieved sorrow and pain.

And God will also weep – and wait.

THE EUCHARIST (COMMUNION)

In Jesus' time, bread and wine were essential, basic elements that sustained physical life. In telling His disciples to remember Him whenever they ate bread and drank wine, Jesus was telling them He (perfect LOVE) is the essential, basic, element of life, and to remember LOVE each time they took essential nourishment for their physical bodies.

SAVING OUR BACON

If we go through life thinking the purpose of life is to save our sorry soul from Hell, we are likely to fail. Such an effort is self-defeating because it focuses our attention on our self and presents God as distant and judgmental. It creates disabling fear and guilt, making God's grace difficult to comprehend and accept.

The purpose of life is to know God (LOVE) well enough to harmonize our life to God (LOVE) and God's creation. One result of accomplishing this is the empowering peace and joy that comes of real-izing (making real) God's (LOVE'S) grace – another result is, we ultimately join God in heaven, saving our sorry soul from Hell.

Isn't it curious? We save our soul by attending to something else.

SOME COMPARISONS.

Following are examples of how Christian beliefs and practices are sometimes understood through the Good/Bad/Reward/Punishment (GBRP) *paradigm and how they are understood differently through the* LOVE *paradigm.*

GOD IS Love

GBRP hears: God is kind and caring.

LOVE hears: God is infinitely perfect LOVE (perfectly Right Spirit, infinite Knowledge, Wisdom, and Power/Action), nothing less – and there is nothing else.

JESUS SAVES

GBRP hears: Christ intervenes with God to undo God's rejection of people. Jesus shields and protects us from God's condemnation and rejection caused by our Sinful nature and sinful deeds. He takes over for us when life becomes more than we can handle.

Love hears: Jesus shows the world how LOVE looks, acts and feels. He frees us from our fear of God, so we can grow in, and connect to, the truth and strength of God's Love and recognize God is always with us and entirely available to us.

ADAM & EVE EVICTED

GBRP hears: God rejected and abandoned them.

Love hears: Adam and Eve came to believe in the idea of good and evil, guiltily hid from God; separated themselves from God. Their guilt and shame made it impossible for them to relate to God as before.

ADAM & EVE TOLD LIFE WILL BE HARD

GBRP hears: God punished them.

Love hears: God told them the facts of living in the outside world, believing in Good and Evil. Then made garments to help them be ready.

PEOPLE ARE MADE IN GOD'S IMAGE

GBRP hears: People are like God's children and are rewarded and punished the way people care for their children.

Love hears: God is perfect Love. People are also Love, but imperfect and limited by our biology, physical bodies, and the physical world we live in.

FAITH

GBRP hears: Varies widely, vaguely defined.

Love hears: An overwhelming, deep, persistent and absolute confidence in Love.

THE GREATEST COMMANDMENT

Love God with all your heart, and all your mind, and all your strength.

GBRP hears: Worship and praise God fervently and faithfully.

Love hears: The greatest commandment is to Love. Love with all your heart (spirit), all your mind (knowledge and wisdom), and all your strength (action). The best thing one can do is to study God (perfect Love), learn everything possible from and about Love, diligently seek to become more familiar with Love, and work to grow Love in oneself and others.

Sin

GBRP hears: God's punishment upon all Adam and Eve's descendants because Adam and Eve gained knowledge of (belief in) good and evil.

Love hears: The fact we fall short of perfect Love due to our physical, mental and emotional limitations, and are restricted to finite knowledge, wisdom, strength, and spirit.

WE ARE BORN IN SIN.

GBRP hears: See previous item.

Love hears: We are born unable to Love perfectly due to the physical, mental and emotional limitations of our bodies.

sin

GBRP hears: Evil manifesting itself in us.

Love hears: Any behavior or attitude that falls short of perfect Love and causes us to shrink from God. Anything that spoils something good.

WE ARE SEPARATED FROM GOD BY Sin.

GBRP hears: God has condemned our Sin (imperfection), and us for bearing it.

Love hears: The physical and social worlds we live in teach us the Good/Bad/Reward/Punishment paradigm, which separates us from God. We fear approaching God because our false "knowledge of right and wrong" gives rise to guilt and expectation of disapproval, judgment, rejection, and punishment.

TRUST JESUS

GBRP hears: Christ will take care of our "problems" if we "believe" fervently enough. Everything will be all right. (Comfortable and as we wish it.)

Love hears: Study, believe, do, and be what Christ taught (Love) and everything will work for good, although not necessarily to our comfort or liking.

HEAVEN

GBRP hears: Reward for "believing in" Jesus and repenting of Sin and sin.

Love hears: Experiencing the full extent of infinite, perfect, Love (God).

HELL

GBRP hears: Punishment for Sin and sin.

Love hears: Becoming fully aware of the past and future impact of our shortcomings without understanding God Loves us and wants us near anyway.

EUCHARIST (COMMUNION)

GBRP hears: Varies widely. Sometimes seen as Christ's body and blood literally reconstituted. Sometimes seen as a reminder Christ died to save us from God's punishment. Sometimes seen as a reminder God loves us.

Love hears: A reminder that every time we take food and drink, essential elements to nourish our physical body, we should remember Love is the essential element of life.

GRACE

GBRP hears: God looks out for us, protects us and guides us whether we deserve it or not.

Love hears: We live immersed in, and saturated by, the Love that is God, no matter what.

Note: *Grace does not mean absence of natural consequences from our actions or inactions.*

NEW

Admiring the line of golden dots around a leaf-green Monarch chrysalis (moths have cocoons), I wondered what the caterpillar inside would look like, shrinking, stretching, and sprouting wings. Curiosity got the best of me. Carefully opening one side of the chrysalis, I was surprised to discover there was no half-modified caterpillar.

Instead, that beautiful green chrysalis was entirely filled with a bright yellow substance, the consistency of raw egg yolk! The caterpillar had, somehow, turned back into its most basic, original material, destined to re-assemble into a gorgeous Monarch butterfly.

I felt both sad and elated. Sad, I had disturbed such a miraculous process. Elated to realize why butterflies are often used as a symbol of resurrection or being "born again." The earth-bound caterpillar would no longer exist, but its essence would become an entirely new creature, flying freely throughout the world.

I'm thinking our essence, Love, is always becoming.

AFTER WORD

I have realized Love is a very old way of understanding life, a paradigm individuals have been discovering and re-discovering for all of time.

For me, the LOVE paradigm is an extremely powerful way of seeing, understanding and responding to the physical and spiritual universe. The LOVE paradigm is free of internal contradictions that often confuse and weaken us, especially those of us unwittingly perceiving the world through a good/bad/reward/punishment paradigm.

It has been a long journey for me. It continues. The LOVE paradigm has been very helpful and the view from here continues to expand. I hope you, also, will be as fortunate.

Live it up! LOVE it all!

Suzanne

LOVE IS NOT OPTIONAL

LOVE is not optional.
It is not a choice.
It is impossible to not LOVE.
The only choice we have,
is to LOVE poorly,
or to LOVE well.

It is a curious thing.

love

is LOVE.

All *is* LOVE.

Their all *is* LOVE.

LOVE *is* all there *is*.

LOVE *is* all there.

LOVE *is* all.

LOVE *is*.

LOVE

Contents

51644448R00152

Made in the USA
Columbia, SC
24 February 2019